Harlequin ┄┄┄┄┄┄┄┄┄┄┄ ent
the ┄┄┄┄┄┄┄┄┄┄┄
award-winning ┄┄┄┄┄┄┄┄┄ n

The
FALCON
D Y N A S T Y

Five successful brothers looking for brides!

Amos Falcon is a proud, self-made man who wants
his legacy to live on through his five sons. Each son
is different, for they have different mothers,
but in one aspect they are the same: their father has
raised them to be ruthless in business and sensible
in matters of the heart.

But one by one these high-achieving brothers will
find that when the right woman comes along,
love is the greatest power of them all….

The next book in The Falcon Dynasty
Plain Jane in the Spotlight will be
available in June 2012.

Dear Reader,

Paris is one of my favourite cities, and I really enjoyed setting a book there. Its beauty and its aura of romance contain a magic that always works for me. Frenchmen, of course, have an especially romantic reputation. An eye for the ladies, appreciation of a pretty face. We love them for it.

Marcel, my hero, seems to be just like that: a man who plays love like a game. But only on the surface. Deep in his heart is a despair that has never left him since he was betrayed by Cassie, his one true love. And when he meets her again it causes an earthquake inside him.

She too is devastated. She was innocent of betrayal, but how can she convince him? The years have changed them. Can their new selves still love as their old selves did? And who are they inside?

I sympathize with that question because it's one that a writer often asks herself. Who am I? Cassie, reaching out to the man who still rules my heart? Or Marcel, trying to resist the love that both alarms and tempts me? The answer, of course, is that I am both, moving between them, and delighted when they find the joy that once seemed lost for ever.

But now they've achieved their happy ending, and it's time for me to become someone else.

Warmest wishes

Lucy Gordon

LUCY GORDON
Miss Prim and the Billionaire

™
Harlequin®

TORONTO NEW YORK LONDON
AMSTERDAM PARIS SYDNEY HAMBURG
STOCKHOLM ATHENS TOKYO MILAN MADRID
PRAGUE WARSAW BUDAPEST AUCKLAND

Recycling programs
for this product may
not exist in your area.

ISBN-13: 978-0-373-17788-2

MISS PRIM AND THE BILLIONAIRE

First North American Publication 2012

Copyright © 2012 by Lucy Gordon

Lucy Gordon cut her writing teeth on magazine journalism, interviewing many of the world's most interesting men, including Warren Beatty, Charlton Heston and Roger Moore. She also camped out with lions in Africa, and had many other unusual experiences, which have often provided the background for her books. Several years ago, while staying in Venice, she met a Venetian who proposed in two days. They have been married ever since. Naturally this has affected her writing, where romantic Italian men tend to feature strongly.

Two of her books have won a Romance Writers of America RITA® Award.

You can visit her website at www.lucy-gordon.com.

Books by Lucy Gordon

RESCUED BY THE BROODING TYCOON*
HIS DIAMOND BRIDE**
A MISTLETOE PROPOSAL**

*The Falcon Dynasty
**Diamonds Are Forever

Other titles by this author available in ebook format.

PROLOGUE

As THE soft light of dawn crept into the room the young man looked down on the girl, asleep beside him, her long blonde hair cascading across the pillow, her face soft and sweet. He kissed her lips gently and she stirred, murmuring, 'Marcel.'

'Shh,' he said. 'I just want to tell you—'

'Mmm?'

'—lots of things. Some of them I can't say when you're awake. When I look at you I'm struck dumb. I can't even find the words to tell you how lovely you are—but then, you already know that.'

He drew the sheet back to reveal her glorious form, both slender and voluptuous.

'There are plenty of people to praise your beauty, those photographers, and so many other men who'd take you from me if they could. But you don't let them. Bless you, my darling, my sweet Cassie.'

Without opening her eyes, she gave a sleepy smile that made Marcel's heart turn over. He was in his early twenties with a face that was still boyish, and as gentle as her own. His naked body was lean, almost too much so. Time would fill out his shape and bring maturity to his features, but perhaps he would never be better than he was now, his dark eyes full of adoration as he gazed down at her.

'Can you hear me? I have something to tell you. You may

be cross with me for concealing it, but you'll forgive me, I know you will. And then I'll ask—no, I'll *beg* you to become my wife. What we have now is wonderful, but I want more. I want to claim you in the sight of the world, to climb to the top of the highest tower and cry aloud that you belong to me. To *me!* Nobody else. We'll marry as soon as possible, won't we, my darling? And all the world will know that you're mine as completely as I am yours.

'That time will come soon, but first I have to explain what I've been hiding. The fact is that I—no, let me keep my secret a little longer. In truth I'm a coward. I'm so afraid that you'll be angry with me when you know that I deceived you, just a little, that I let you think—never mind. I'll tell you when the right moment comes.

'For this moment I just want to say that I love you, I belong to you, and nothing will ever part us. My darling, if you knew how I long to call you my wife. I pray that our wedding will happen soon.

'But sleep now, just a little longer. There'll be time later. We have all our lives to love each other.'

CHAPTER ONE

'THE trouble with weddings is that they bring out the idiot in people.'

The cynical remark made Marcel Falcon glance up, grinning with agreement. The man who'd come to sit beside him was a business associate with whom he was on cordial terms.

'Good to see you, Jeremy,' he said. 'I'll get the drinks. Waiter!'

They were at a table in the bar of the Gloriana Hotel, one of the most luxurious establishments in London, providing not only rooms but wedding facilities for those who could afford them. Marcel gave his order, signed for it to go onto his bill and turned back to his companion, saying, 'You're right about weddings. No good to anyone. I'd just as soon have avoided this one, but my brother, Darius, is the bride's ex-husband.'

Jeremy stared. 'And he's a guest at her wedding to another man? I've heard of sophisticated, but that takes the biscuit.'

'It's for the children, Frankie and Mark. They need to see their parents acting friendly despite the divorce.'

'And I'll bet your father had a hand in the decision.'

'There aren't many decisions my father doesn't have a hand in,' Marcel agreed wryly. 'He actually got them to delay the wedding until a certain date had passed, so that he could come to England without incurring a huge tax bill.'

Amos Falcon was so extravagantly wealthy that he'd had to flee to the tax haven of Monaco where he lived for most of the time, venturing back to England for only ninety days of the year.

'Frankie and Mark are his only grandchildren,' Marcel said, 'so he's determined to stay part of their lives.'

'Strange, that. A man with five sons and only one of them has carried on the line so far.'

'He says the same thing. He's always urging us to marry, preferably Freya.'

'Who's Freya?'

'His stepdaughter, the closest thing to a daughter that he has, and he's set on marrying her to one of us, and so binding her into the family.'

'Don't any of you get a say in your choice of wife?'

'Are you kidding? This is my father we're talking about. Since when did anyone ever get a say?' Marcel spoke cynically but with wry affection.

'Failing Freya,' he went on, 'then some other wife to continue the great Falcon dynasty. But except for Darius we've all disappointed him. Jackson seems to find wild animals more interesting than people, Leonid is a man we hardly ever see. He could have a dozen wives, but since he seldom leaves Russia we wouldn't know. And Travis doesn't dare marry. He'd lose all his fans.'

He spoke of his younger half-brother, born and raised in America, and a successful television actor with an army of adoring female followers.

'No man could be expected to risk his fortune just for marriage,' Jeremy agreed solemnly. 'That just leaves you, the amorous Frenchman.'

Marcel grimaced. 'Enough!' he said. 'If you knew how that stereotype bores me.'

'And yet you make use of it. The life in Paris, the endless

supply of women—all right, all right.' He broke off hastily, seeing Marcel's face. 'But since you have what most men would give their eye teeth for, the least you can do is enjoy it.'

The waiter arrived with their drinks. When he'd gone Jeremy raised his glass.

'Here's to being a bachelor. I'd give a lot to know how you've managed to stay single so long.'

'A sense of reality helps. You start off regarding all women as goddesses, but you soon see reason.'

'Ah! Let you down with a crash, did she?'

'I can't remember,' Marcel said coldly. 'She no longer exists.'

She never really did, said the voice in his head. *A figment of your imagination.*

'Well, I reckon you've got it right,' Jeremy said. 'All the women you want, whenever you want.'

'Stop talking nonsense.'

'I'm not. Look at those girls. They can't keep their eyes off you.'

It was true. Three young women were at the bar, buying drinks then glancing around, seeming to take stock of the men, form opinions about them, each pausing when they came to Marcel. One of them drew a long breath, one put her head on one side, and the third gave an inviting smile.

You couldn't blame them, Jeremy reckoned, Marcel was in his thirties, tall, dark-haired and well built but without a spare ounce on him anywhere. His face was handsome enough to make the girls swoon and the men want to commit murder.

But it was more than looks. Marcel had a charm that was delightful or deadly, depending on your point of view. Those who'd encountered only that charisma found it hard to believe in the ruthlessness with which he'd stormed the heights of wealth and success—until they encountered that ruthlessness for themselves. And were floored by it.

But the willing females at the bar knew nothing of this. They saw Marcel's looks, the seemingly roguish gleam in his eyes, and they responded. Soon, Jeremy guessed, at least one of them would find an excuse to approach him. Or perhaps all three.

'Have you made your choice?' he asked caustically.

'I don't like to rush it.'

'Ah yes, of course. And there are some more just coming in. Hey, isn't that Darius?'

The door of the bar led into the hotel lobby, where they could just see Marcel's half-brother, Darius Falcon, pressing the button at the elevator. A young woman stood beside him, talking eagerly.

'Who's she?' Jeremy asked.

'I don't know,' Marcel replied. 'I think she comes from the island he's just acquired. A man who owed him money used it to pay the debt, and he's living there at the moment while he decides what to do. He told me he'd be bringing someone, but he didn't say a lot about her.'

By now Darius and his companion had stepped into the elevator and the doors had closed.

'I must go up and greet them,' Marcel said, draining his glass. 'See you later.'

It was an excuse. Before visiting Darius he meant to call on their father, who'd arrived an hour ago. But instead of heading straight for the main suite, he strolled about, inspecting his surroundings with the eye of a professional. The Gloriana might be among the top hotels in London but it couldn't compete with La Couronne, the hotel he owned in Paris.

He'd named it La Couronne, the crown, to let the world know that it was the queen of hotels, and his own pride and joy. He had personally overseen every detail of an establishment that offered conference facilities as well as luxurious accommodation, discretion as well as flamboyance. Anybody who was anybody had stayed there: top level businessmen, politicians, film stars. It was a place of fashion and influence. But most of all money.

Money was the centre of his life. And from that centre it stretched out its tentacles to every distant detail. He'd started his business with loans guaranteed by his father, who also added money of his own, to be repaid in due course. Marcel had returned every penny.

At the back of the hotel he found a huge room that would be used for the wedding next day. It was a grandiose place, decorated to imitate a church, although the ceremony would be a civil one. Flowers were being piled everywhere, suggesting a romantic dream.

'We'll marry as soon as possible, won't we, my darling? And all the world will know that you're mine as completely as I am yours.'

The voice that echoed in his head made him stiffen and take an involuntary step back, as though seeking escape.

But the voice was his own and there was nowhere to flee.

'If you knew how I long to call you my wife.'

Had he really said that? Had he actually been that stupid? Young, naïve, believing what he longed to believe about the girl he adored, until his delusions were stripped away in pain and misery.

But that was long past. Now he was a different man. If only the voice would stop tormenting him.

He left the wedding venue quickly and almost at once bumped into his father. They had last met several weeks ago when Amos had suffered heart trouble, causing his sons to hurry to his bedside in Monaco. Now, to Marcel's relief, the old man seemed strong again. His face had aged with the strain of his illness, but he was both vigorous and alert.

'Good to see you better,' he said, embracing his father unselfconsciously.

'Nothing wrong with me,' Amos declared robustly. 'Just a lot of fuss. But I was glad to have you all there for a while. Now you must come up and visit Janine and Freya. They're looking forward to seeing you again.'

Amos's private life might politely be described as colourful. Marcel's mother had been his second wife. Janine was his third. Freya, her daughter by a previous husband, was also part of the family. Amos, a man with five sons and no daughters, had particularly welcomed her as a plan formed in his mind.

'Let's go up slowly,' he suggested now. 'We can take a look at the place and get some ideas. It's not a bad hotel but you could do better.'

'I've been thinking of expanding,' Marcel mused. 'A change of scene might be interesting.'

'Then London's the place to look. Property prices have plunged and you could pick up a bargain. I've got some good banking contacts who'll help, and I can loan you some money myself, if needed.'

'Thanks. I might take you up on that.'

They toured the hotel, each making notes.

'The one thing this place has got that La Couronne hasn't is the wedding facility,' Amos observed. 'You might try that. Money to be made.'

'I doubt if it would increase my profit,' Marcel said coolly. There were many reasons why weddings didn't appeal to him, but none that he was prepared to discuss.

They finished on the eighth floor where there was a bar with magnificent views of London. Sitting by the window, Amos indicated a tall building in the distance.

'See that? Headquarters of Daneworth Estates.'

'I've heard of them,' Marcel mused. 'Things not going too well, I gather.'

'That's right. They're having to sell assets.'

Amos's tone held a significance that made Marcel ask, 'Any asset in particular?'

'The Alton Hotel. It was bought with the idea of development but the money ran out and it's ripe for takeover at a knock-down price.'

He quoted a figure and Marcel's eyebrows rose. 'As little as that?'

'It's possible, if someone with a certain amount of influence twisted the screw on Daneworth so that the sale became more urgent.'

'You don't happen to know anyone with that kind of influence?' Marcel asked satirically.

'I might. How long will you be in England?'

'Long enough to look around.'

'Excellent.' Amos made a noise that sounded like 'Hrmph!' adding, 'It's good to know I have one son I can be proud of.'

'Are you still mad at Darius because he gave his wife too generous a deal over the divorce? I thought you liked Mary. You've come to her wedding.'

'I won't quarrel with the mother of my only grandchildren. But sense is sense, and he hasn't shown any. Do you know anything about the girl he's bringing with him today?'

'I saw them arrive. She looks attractive and pleasant. I'm going to visit them in a minute.'

'While you're there take a good look at her. See if Darius is falling into her trap.'

'Thus spoiling your scheme to marry him to Freya?' Marcel said ironically.

'I'd like to have Freya as my daughter-in-law, I make no secret of it. And if Darius won't come up to the mark—'

'Forget it,' Marcel interrupted him.

'Why should I? It's time you were putting down roots.'

'There are plenty of others to do that.'

Amos snorted. 'Five sons! Five! You'd think more than one of you would have settled down by now.'

But Amos himself was hardly an advertisement for domesticity, Marcel thought cynically. Of the five sons, only two had been born to the woman he'd been married to at the time. His own mother hadn't married Amos until several years after his birth. Travis and Leonid were bastards and proud of it. But he didn't want to quarrel with his father, so he merely shrugged and rose to go.

'Tell Janine and Freya I'll be up as soon as I've been to see Darius,' he said.

As he approached his brother's room he was barely conscious of adjusting his mask. He donned it so often that it was second nature by now, even with a brother with whom he was on cordial terms. When he arrived his charming smile was firmly in place.

The door was already open, giving him a clear view of a pretty young woman, done up in a glamorous style, and Darius regarding her with admiration, his hands on her shoulders.

'Am I interrupting anything?' he asked.

'Marcel!' Darius advanced to thump his brother with delight, after which he turned and introduced his companion as Harriet.

'You've been keeping this lady a big secret,' Marcel said, regarding her with admiration. 'And I understand why. If she were mine I would also hide her away from the world.'

His father was in for a shock, he reckoned. Harriet was definitely a threat to his plans for Darius's next wife.

He chatted with her for a few moments, flirting, but not beyond brotherly limits.

'So Darius has warned you about the family,' he said at last, 'and you know we're a load of oddities.'

'I'll bet you're no odder than me,' she teased.

'I'll take you up on that. Promise me a dance tonight.'

'She declines,' Darius said firmly.

Marcel chuckled and murmured in Harriet's ear, 'We'll meet again later.'

After a little more sparring, he blew her a kiss and departed, heading for his father's suite. He greeted his stepmother cordially but he couldn't help looking over her shoulder at the window, through which he could see the building Amos had pointed out to him.

Daneworth Estates. Assets ripe for an offer. Interesting.

In an office on the tenth floor of a bleakly efficient building overlooking the River Thames, Mr Smith, the manager of Daneworth Estates, examined some papers and groaned before raising his voice to call, 'Mrs Henshaw, can you bring the other files in, please?'

He turned back to his client, a middle-aged man, saying, 'She'll have all the details. Don't worry.'

He glanced up as a young woman appeared in the doorway and advanced with the files.

'I've made notes,' she said. 'I think you'll find I've covered everything.'

'I'm sure you have,' he replied.

The client regarded her with distaste. She was exactly the kind of woman he most disliked, the kind who could have looked better if she'd bothered to make the best of herself. She had the advantage of being tall and slim, with fair hair and regular features. But she scraped her hair back, dressed severely, and concealed her face behind a pair of large steel-rimmed spectacles.

'It's nearly six o'clock,' she said.

Mr Smith nodded. 'Yes, you can go.'

She gave the client a faint nod and left the office.
He shivered. 'She terrifies me,' he admitted.

'Me too, sometimes,' Mr Smith agreed. 'But if there's one
person whose efficiency I can rely on it's Mrs Henshaw.'

'It always sounds odd to me the way you call her "Mrs".
Why not just Jane?'

'She prefers it. Familiarity is something she discourages.'

'But you're her boss.'

'Sometimes I wonder which of us is the boss. I hesitate
between valuing her skills and wanting to get rid of her.'

'She reminds me of a robot.'

'She certainly doesn't have any "come hither" about her,'
the manager agreed. 'You'd never think she'd once been a
fashion model.'

'Get away!'

'Really. She was called "Cassie" and for a couple of years
she was headed for the very top. Then it all ended. I'm not
sure why.'

'She could still look good if she tried,' the client observed.
'Why scrape her hair back against her skull like a prison
wardress? And when did you last see a woman who didn't
bother with make-up?'

'Can't think! Now, back to business. How do I avoid going
bankrupt and taking your firm down with me?'

'Can't think!' the client echoed gloomily.

Neither of them gave a further thought to Mrs Henshaw
on the far side of the door. She heard their disparaging com-
ments and shrugged.

'Blimey!' said the other young woman in the room. 'How
do you stand them being so rude about you?'

Her name was Bertha. She was nineteen, naïve, friendly
and a reasonably good secretary.

'I ignore it,' Mrs Henshaw said firmly.

'But who was that Cassie they keep on about? The gorgeous model.'

'No idea. She was nothing to do with me, I know that.'

'But they said it was you.'

'They were wrong.' Mrs Henshaw turned to look at Bertha with a face that was blank and lifeless. 'Frankly,' she said, 'Cassie never really existed. Now hurry off home.'

The last words had an edge of desperation. She urgently needed to be alone to think about everything that was happening. She knew the company was in dire straits, and it would soon be time to move on.

But to what? Her life seemed to stretch before her, blank, empty. Just as it had done for the last ten years.

The days when she could afford a car were over, and she took a bus to the small block of apartments where she lived in a few rooms one floor up. Here everything was neat, restrained, unrevealing. A nun might have lived in this place.

Tonight was no different from any other night, she assured herself. The name Cassie, suddenly screaming out of the darkness, had thrown the world into chaos, but she'd recovered fast. Cassie was another life, another universe. Cassie's heart had been broken. Mrs Henshaw had no heart to break.

She stayed up late studying papers, understanding secrets about the firm that were supposed to be hidden. Soon there would have to be decisions but now she was too weary in her soul to think about them.

She was asleep as soon as her head hit the pillow, but it wasn't a peaceful sleep. The dreams she'd dreaded were waiting to pounce. There was Cassie, gloriously naked, madly in love, throwing herself into the arms of the handsome boy who'd worshipped her. There were his eyes, gazing at her with adoration, but then with hate.

'I loved you—I trusted you—now I can't bear the sight of you!'

In sleep she reached out her hands to him, crying, 'Marcel, you don't understand—please—please—'

'Get out of my sight! *Whore!*'

She screamed and awoke to find herself thrashing around in bed, throwing her head from side to side.

'No,' she cried. 'It isn't true. *No, no, no!'*

Then she was sitting up, staring into the darkness, heaving violently.

'Leave me alone,' she begged. 'Leave me alone.'

Wearily she got out of bed and stumbled into the bathroom. A shambling wreck of a woman looked back at her from the mirror. Now the severe barriers of the day were gone, leaving no trace of the steely 'prison wardress'. The tense stillness of her face was replaced by violent emotion that threatened to overwhelm and destroy her. Her hair, no longer scraped back, flowed over her shoulders, giving her a cruel resemblance to Cassie, the beautiful girl who had lived long ago. That girl had vanished into the mists, but suddenly her likeness taunted Mrs Henshaw from the mirror. Tears streamed from her eyes and she covered them with her hands, seeking oblivion.

'No,' she wept. 'No!'

But it was too late to say no. Years too late.

CHAPTER TWO

'I JUST hope I don't regret this,' Mr Smith said heavily. 'The Alton Hotel is worth twice what he's offering, but it's still the best offer we've had.'

Mrs Henshaw was frowning as she studied the figures. 'Surely you can drive him up a little?'

'I tried to but he just said "Take it or leave it." So I took it. We have to sell off properties fast, before we go under.'

'Is that your way of telling me to find another job?'

'Yes, but I may be able to help you. I've told him you'll meet him to discuss details. Marcel needs an assistant with local knowledge, so I'm sure you can impress him. Why are you looking like that?'

'Nothing—nothing—what did you say his name was?'

'Marcel Falcon. He's one of Amos Falcon's sons.'

She relaxed, telling herself to be sensible. The Marcel she had known had been Marcel Degrande, and obviously no connection with this man. It was absurd to be still reacting to the name after so long.

'Play your cards right and you'll come out on top,' Mr Smith advised.

'When do I go?'

'Right now. He's staying at the Gloriana Hotel, and he's expecting you there in half an hour.'

'Half a—? *What?* But that doesn't give me time to research the background or the man—'

'You'll have to play it by ear. And these papers—' he thrust some at her '—will give you the details of his offer. Yes, I know we don't usually do it like this, but things are moving fast and the sooner we get the money the better.'

She took a taxi and spent the journey memorising facts and figures, wishing she'd had time to do some online research. She'd heard of Amos Falcon, whose financial tentacles seemed to stretch halfway across the world, but it would have been useful to check his son out too.

Never mind, she thought. A heavy evening's work lay ahead of her, and she would tackle it with the meticulous efficiency that now ruled her whole life.

At last she entered the Gloriana and approached the reception desk. 'Please tell Mr Falcon that Mrs Jane Henshaw is here.'

'He's over there, madam.'

Turning, she saw the entrance door to the bar and just inside, a man sitting at a table. At that moment he turned his head, revealing just enough of his face to leave her stunned.

'No,' she whispered. 'No…no…'

The world went into chaos, thundering to a halt, yet still whirling mysteriously about her.

Marcel. Older, a little heavier, yet still the man whose love had been the glorious triumph of her life, and whose loss had brought her close to destruction. What malign chance had made their paths cross again?

She took a step back, then another, moving towards the door, desperate to escape before he saw her. She managed to get into the hotel garden where there was a small café, and sat down. She was shaking too violently to leave now. She must stay here for a while.

If only he hadn't seen her.

If only they had never seen each other in the beginning, never met, never loved, never hated, never shattered each other.

Who were those two youngsters who seemed to stand before her now? Naïve, innocent, ignorant, perhaps a little stupid, but only with the stupidity of children who knew they could conquer the world with their beauty, talent and enthusiasm.

Jane Agnes Cassandra Baines had always known she was destined to be a model.

'Nobody could be that beautiful and waste it,' her sister had said. 'Go for it, girl. And choose a better name. Jane will make people think of plain Jane.'

Rebecca was eight years her senior, and had been almost her mother since their parents died in their childhood. These days Rebecca's misfortunes meant that she was the one who needed caring for, and much of Jane's money went in helping her.

'Cassandra,' Rebecca had said back then. 'Mum loved that name because she said it meant "enticer of men". Dad was outraged. I can still remember them squabbling, him saying, "You can't call her that. It's not respectable." In the end Mum managed to squeeze it in as your third name.'

'Enticer of men,' she'd murmured in delight. 'Cassandra. Yes—I'm Cassandra.'

Her agent had partly agreed. 'Not Cassandra, Cassie,' he said. 'It's perfect. You're going to be a star.'

She'd climbed fast. Jane no longer existed. Cassie's picture was everywhere and so were her admirers. Wealthy men had laid their golden gifts at her feet, but she'd cared only for Marcel Degrande, a poor boy who lived in a shabby flat.

He'd been earning a pittance working for a grocery store, and they'd met when he'd delivered fruit to her door. One look at his smile, his teasing eyes, and she'd tossed aside two millionaires like unwanted rubbish. From then on there was only him.

For Marcel it had been the same. Generous, passionate, he had offered himself to her, heart and soul, with nothing held back.

'I can't believe this is happening,' he said. 'You could have them and their money, but me—you've seen how I live. I can't take you to posh restaurants or buy you expensive presents.'

'But you give me something no other man can give,' she assured him, laying her hand over his heart. 'Who cares about money? Money's boring.'

'Yes. Money is boring,' he said fervently. 'Who needs it?'

'Nobody.' She threw herself back on the bed and wriggled luxuriously. 'But there's something I do need, and I'm getting impatient.'

'Your wish is my command,' he said just before his mouth came down on hers, his hands explored her willing body, and they quickly became one.

Returning his love had been the greatest joy of her life, a joy that she knew instinctively could never be repeated. It had lasted a few months, then ended in cruelty.

Jake, a rich, powerful man with criminal connections, used to getting his own way, had made it plain that he wanted her. She'd told him he had no chance. He'd departed without a word, and she'd congratulated herself on having dealt with the situation.

Marcel had been away making a long-distance delivery. When he called she said nothing about Jake, not wanting to worry him. Time enough to tell him everything when he returned.

He never did return. On the evening she expected him the hours passed without a word. She tried to call, but his phone was dead. At last there was a knock on her door and there was Jake.

He thrust a photograph into her hands. It showed Marcel in bed, bloodied, bandaged and barely alive.

'He had an accident,' Jake said, smirking. 'A van knocked him over in the street.'

'Oh, heavens, I must go to him. Which hospital is he in?'

'You don't need to know that. You're not going to see him again. Are you getting the message yet? I could have him killed in a moment, and I will if you don't see sense. And don't even try to find the hospital and visit him because I'll know, and he'll pay the price.'

He pointed to the picture. 'A doctor who works there owes me a favour. She took this. I'm sure you don't want him to suffer any more…misfortunes.'

She was left with the knowledge that not only was Marcel badly hurt and she could never see him again, but that he would think she had deserted him. That thought nearly destroyed her.

She risked writing him a letter, telling everything, swearing her love, begging him not to hate her, and slipped it through the door of his dingy apartment. He would find it when he returned from the hospital.

For days she waited, certain that Marcel would contact her, however briefly. But he never did, and the deafening silence blotted out the world. His phone stayed dead. In desperation, she called his landlady, who confirmed that she'd seen him arrive home and collect mail from the carpet.

'Ask him to call me,' she begged.

'I can't. He's vanished, just packed his bags and left. I think he still has some family in France, so maybe he's gone there. Or maybe not. His mobile phone's dead and it's like he never existed.'

But it was the other way around, she thought in agony. Marcel had wiped *her* out as though she'd never existed. Obviously he didn't believe her explanation that she had done it for him. Or if he did believe, it made no difference. He hated her and he would not forgive.

Now his voice spoke in her memory.

'It's all or nothing with me, and with you it's all, my beloved Cassie. Everything, always.'

And she'd responded eagerly, *'Always, always—'*

But he'd warned her, all or nothing. And now it was nothing.

Sitting in the hotel garden, she tried to understand what she'd just learned. The 'poor boy' with barely a penny had actually been the son of a vastly wealthy man. But perhaps he hadn't known. He might have been illegitimate and only discovered his father later. She must try to believe that because otherwise their whole relationship had been based on a lie. The love and open-heartedness, so sweet between them, would have been an illusion.

She shivered.

It was time to flee before he found her. She couldn't bear to meet him and see his eyes as he discovered her now, her looks gone. How he would gloat at her downfall, how triumphant he would be in his revenge.

But as she neared the building she saw that it was already too late. The glass door into the garden was opening. Marcel was there, and with him the receptionist, saying, 'There's the lady, sir. I was sure I saw her come out here. Mrs Henshaw, here is Mr Falcon.'

'I'm sorry I kept you waiting,' Marcel said smoothly.

'No…it was my fault,' she stammered. 'I shouldn't have come outside—'

'I don't blame you at all. It's stifling in there, isn't it? Why don't we both sit out in the fresh air?'

He gestured towards the garden and she walked ahead, too dazed to do anything else.

He hadn't reacted.

He hadn't recognised her.

It might be the poor light. Twilight was settling, making everything fade into shadows, denying him a clear view of her face. That was a relief. It would give her time to take control of the situation.

But she was shaken with anguish as they reached a table and he pulled out a chair for her. He had loved her so much, and now he no longer recognised her.

'What can I get you to drink?' Marcel asked. 'Champagne?'

'Tonic water, please,' she said. 'I prefer to keep a clear head.'

'You're quite right. I'll have the same since obviously I'd better keep a clear head too. Waiter!'

A stranger might be fooled by this, she thought wryly, but the young Marcel had had an awesome ability to imbibe cheap wine while losing none of his faculties. After a night of particular indulgence she'd once challenged him to prove that he was 'up to it'. Whereupon he'd tossed her onto the bed, flung himself down beside her and proved it again and again, to the delight and hilarity of them both.

Hilarity? Yes. It had been a joy and a joke at the same time—exhausting each other, triumphing over each other, never knowing who was the winner, except that they both were.

'Cassie, my sweet beloved, why do you tease me?'

'To get you to do what I wanted, of course.'

'And did I do it to your satisfaction?'

'Let's try again and I'll let you know.'

'You clearly believe that business comes before pleasure,' he told her now in a voice that the years hadn't changed. He spoke English well, but with the barest hint of a French accent that had always enchanted her.

How many women, she wondered, had been enchanted by it since?

'Smith recommended you to me in the highest possible terms,' Marcel continued. 'He said nobody knew as much about my new property as you.'

'I hope I can live up to Mr Smith's praise,' she said primly.

'I'm sure you will.' His reply was courteous and mechanical.

'Do you mean to make the hotel similar to La Couronne?'

'I see you've been doing your homework. Excellent. There will be similarities. I aim to provide many facilities, like a conference centre.'

'I wonder if the building is big enough for that.'

'I agree. There will need to be expansion. I want the best firm of builders you can recommend.'

For a while he continued to talk about his plans, which were ambitious, and she made notes, not even raising her head when the waiter appeared with their tonic water.

Her hand, and one part of her brain, were working automatically. There was nothing in him to suggest recognition, no tension, no brightening of the eyes. His oblivion was so total that she even wondered if she was mistaken and he wasn't her Marcel after all. But when she stole a sideways glance she knew there had been no mistake. The shape of his head, the curve of his lips, the darkness of his eyes; all these she knew, even at a distance of years.

This was her Marcel.

Yet no longer hers.

And no longer really Marcel.

The same was true of her. Cassie was gone for ever and only Mrs Henshaw remained.

He moved and she hastened to bury herself in her work. When she dared to look up he had filled her glass. In her best businesslike voice she said, 'I happen to know that the owner of the building next door has been thinking of selling.'

'That would be useful for my expansion. Give me the details and I'll approach him. Do you have any more information?'

She scribbled some details and passed them to him.

'Excellent. I'm sure Smith told you that I need an assistant to work with me on this project. You'd do better than anyone.'

'That's very impulsive. Don't you need more time to think about it?'

'Not at all. The right decisions are very quickly made. And so they should be.'

For a moment she was fired with temptation. To take the job, be with him day after day, with him not knowing who she was. The prospect was so enticing as to be scary.

But she could not. She *must* not.

'It's impossible,' she said reluctantly.

'Why? Would your husband object? He doesn't mind you working for Smith.'

'I'm divorced.'

'So you're the mistress of your own destiny and can do as you choose.'

She almost laughed aloud. Once she'd imagined exactly the same, and been shown otherwise in the most brutal fashion.

'Nobody chooses their own destiny,' she said. 'We only think we do. Wise people remember that.'

He gave her a curious look. 'Are you wise, Mrs Henshaw?'

'Sooner or later we all become wise, don't we?'

'Some of us.'

As he said it he looked directly at her. She met his eyes, seeking recognition in them, but seeing only a blank. Or merely a weariness and disillusion that matched her own.

'Things are moving fast in the property world,' he said, 'as I'm sure you know. When I tell Smith that I've decided to employ you I'm sure he'll release you quickly.'

He'd decided, she noted. No suggestion that she had a decision to make.

'I need a little time to think,' she hedged.

'I'll pay you twice what you're getting now.'

'I could lie about the amount.'

'And I could check with him. I won't, though, I trust you. Don't worry, I'm a hard taskmaster. I'll get full value from you.'

'Now, look—'

'I won't take no for an answer. Fine, that's settled.'

'It is not,' she said, her temper rising. 'Please don't try to tell me what to do.'

'As your employer I shall expect to.'

'But you're not my employer.'

'I soon will be.'

He'd always liked his own way, she recalled, but he'd used charm. Now charm was gone, replaced by bullying. Perhaps she couldn't entirely blame him after the way he'd suffered. But still she knew she had to escape.

'Mr Falcon, I think it's time you understood—'

'Well, well, well. Who'd have thought it?'

The words, coming out of nowhere, startled them both. Approaching them was a large man with an air of pathological self-satisfaction.

'Oh, no,' she groaned. 'Not him.'

'You know this man?'

'He's Keith Lanley, part financial journalist, part muckraker. He spends his days scurrying around trying to work out who's going to go bankrupt next.'

'What a thing to happen!' Lanley exclaimed, coming up to them. 'So the rumours are true, Jane. You're a sly character, getting out of Daneworth while the going's good. Aren't you going to introduce me to your friend? Of course I already know who he is. Everyone's ears pricked up when the Falcon family came to town.'

'I'm here for a wedding,' Marcel said coldly. 'So are the other members of my family.'

'Of course, of course. But no Falcon ever passed up the chance of making money, now, did he? And a lot depends on how you present it to the world. Suppose we three—'

But she'd had enough.

'Goodbye,' she said, rising to her feet.

'Now, wait—'

Lanley reached to grab her but she evaded him and fled deeper into the garden. Trying to follow her, Lanley found himself detained by Marcel, his face dark with rage.

'Leave her alone,' he said furiously.

'Hey, no need to get irate. I could do you a favour.'

'The only favour you could do me is to vanish off the face of the earth. Now, get out before I have you arrested.'

'I suppose you could, too,' Lanley said in a resigned voice. 'All right, I'll go—for now.' He began to go but turned. 'You couldn't just give me a quote about your father?'

'Get out!'

When the man had departed Marcel looked around. He was breathing hard, trying to force himself to be calm when all he wanted to do was roar to the heavens. Anguish possessed him, but more than anguish was rage—terrifying anger at her, at himself, at the cruel fate that had allowed this to happen.

Where was she? Vanished into thin air?

Again!

He began to run, hunting her here and there until at last he came across her leaning against a tree, her back to him. He touched her and her reaction was instant and violent.

'No, leave me alone. I won't talk to you.'

'It's not Lanley, I've sent him away.'

But she didn't seem to hear, fending him off madly until she lost her balance and fell, knocking her head against the tree. He tried to catch her but could only partly break her fall, steadying her as she slid to the ground.

'Your head,' he said hoarsely. *'Cassie.'*

People were approaching, calling out.

'She's collapsed,' he called back. 'She needs a doctor.'

Lifting her in his arms, he hurried the hundred yards back to the hotel. Word had gone ahead and the hotel doctor was waiting for them.

Her eyes were closed but she was aware of everything, especially Marcel's arms holding her firmly. Where their bodies touched she could feel his warmth, and just sense the soft thunder of his heart.

Cassie. He'd called her Cassie.

Hadn't he?

Her mind was swimming. Through the confusion she could hear his voice crying 'Cassie,' but had he said it or had she imagined it through the fog of her agitation? Had he known her all the time and concealed it? What would he do now?

She felt herself laid down and heard voices above her. She gave a soft gasp and opened her eyes.

'I think Mrs Henshaw's coming round,' the doctor said.

Marcel's face hovered over her.

'I'm all right, honestly,' she murmured. 'I just bumped my head against the tree and it made me dizzy for a moment.'

'Let's do a check,' the doctor said.

She barely heard. Her eyes were seeking Marcel's face, desperate to know what she could read in it.

But it was blank. There was nothing there.

For a moment she fought the truth, but then she forced herself to accept it. He hadn't recognised her, hadn't spoken her name. She'd simply imagined what she wanted to believe.

No!

A thousand voices screamed denial in her head. That wasn't what she wanted. She wouldn't think it or allow him to think it.

The doctor finished checking her, cleaned the graze and pronounced himself satisfied. 'But I'd recommend an early night,' he said. 'Are you staying here?'

'No.'

'Does anyone live at home with you?'

'No.'

'Pity. I'd rather you weren't alone tonight.'

'She won't be,' Marcel intervened. 'She'll stay in my suite, with a woman to watch out for her.'

'Oh, will I?' she said indignantly.

'Yes, Mrs Henshaw. You will. Please don't waste my time with further argument.'

He walked out, leaving her seething. *'Cheek!'*

'Be fair,' said the doctor. 'He obviously cares a lot about you.'

'Not at all. I've only just met him.'

In a few minutes it was clear that Marcel had gone to make arrangements. He returned with a wheelchair.

'I don't need that,' she said, aghast.

'Yes, you do. Take my hand.'

This was the moment to hurry away, put the whole disastrous evening behind her and forget that Marcel had ever existed. But he had firm hold of her, ushering her into the chair in a manner that brooked no refusal.

Since arguing was useless she sat in silence as he took her into the elevator and upstairs to his suite, where a pleasant-looking young woman was waiting.

'This is my sister Freya,' he said.

'I've brought you a nightdress,' Freya said.

'I'll leave you.' Marcel departed quickly.

'This is the bedroom and bathroom,' Freya told her. 'I'll

look in often to make sure you're all right. Let me help you undress.'

As they worked on it Freya asked, 'Whatever did Marcel do to you?'

'It wasn't his fault. I fell against a tree.'

'Well, he obviously feels responsible.'

'He has no need.'

'Perhaps he's just a very generous and responsible man. I'm still getting to know him.'

'I thought he said you were his sister.'

'His stepsister.' Freya laughed. 'He keeps calling me his sister so that he doesn't have to marry me.'

'What?'

'Amos wants me to marry one of his sons so that I'll really be part of the family. His first choice is Darius but Darius is no more keen than I am. So then Marcel is "next in the firing line" as he puts it. That "sister" business is his way of protecting himself.'

'How do you feel about that?'

Freya chuckled. 'I'm not weeping into my pillow. He's not my style at all. Too much like his father. Oh, it's rotten of me to say that when Amos has been so kind to me, but now I can still escape. The thought of being married to a man like that—' She gave a melodramatic shudder.

'Like what?'

'Money, money, money. That and always being one step ahead of his enemies.'

'Does Marcel have a lot of enemies?'

'I've no idea. I don't think he has many friends. There's a coldness in him that it's hard to get past. There now, you're ready for bed. Would you like me to stay?'

'No, thank you. You've been very kind.'

She was desperate to be alone. As soon as the door closed

she pulled the covers over her head and tried to sort out her confused mind.

Freya had spoken of his coldness, but the young man she'd known and loved had been incapable of coldness. Somehow, one had become the other.

This isn't happening. It can't be. I'll wake up and find it was a dream. At least, I hope so. Or do I hope so? Is that what I really want? Did he recognise me or not? Is he just pretending not to? What am I hoping for?

But thinking was too troubling, so at last she gave up and fell asleep.

CHAPTER THREE

SHE awoke suddenly in the dark. Listening intently, she could make out the sound of footsteps nearing her room. Marcel. She slid further down the bed, pulling the duvet over her, not sure that she wanted to see him.

The door opened, someone came in and stood looking down at her. Her heart was thundering as the moment of truth neared. Last night he'd seemed not to know her, but then she'd heard her name whispering past. Surely that had come from him and now everything was different. What would he say to her? What could she say to him?

She gasped as a hand touched her.

'It's only me,' said Freya. 'I'm sorry, did I wake you?'

'No, no, I…I'm all right.' She didn't know what she was saying. Everything was spinning in chaos.

Freya switched on the lamp and sat down on the bed, placing a cup on the sidetable.

'I'm going now, but I brought you a cup of tea first.'

'Thank you.'

'Jane—do you mind if I call you Jane? Or should it be Mrs Henshaw?'

'Oh, please, no.' She shuddered. 'I've had enough of Mrs Henshaw.'

'Jane, then?'

'Yes, Jane. Although I think I've had enough of Jane too.'

'Goodness, what does that mean?' Freya's friendliness was charming.

'Suddenly I seem to be a lot of different people and none of them is really me. Does that sound crazy?'

'Not in this family,' Freya said wryly. 'You have to be a bit crazy to get your head around the way they all live. Sometimes I worry for my mother. She's Amos's third wife and he wasn't faithful to either of the others.'

'Where does Marcel come in the picture?' Jane Henshaw asked, careful to drink her tea at once to hide her face.

'When Amos was married to Elaine, Darius's mother, he travelled abroad a lot, and while he was doing business in France he met Laura, set up home with her and they had Marcel.'

'While he was still married to Elaine?'

'While he was still actually living with her in England. He divided his time between London and Paris, and even had another son by his wife. That's Jackson. A couple of years later Elaine found out about his infidelity and left him. He brought Laura and Marcel over to England and married her as soon as his divorce was through.'

'So Marcel grew up in England?' Jane said slowly.

'I think he was about eleven when he moved here. Of course it didn't last. When he was fifteen Laura discovered that Amos had been "at it" again, and she returned to Paris, taking Marcel with her. He came back seven years later, but not to Amos. He resented the way his mother had been treated, and he even stopped using the name Falcon and went back to using Laura's name, Degrande.

'He had a rebellious streak and set up home with some other lads, living from day to day, doing any job they could get. He enjoyed it for a couple of years, then went back to France. Eventually he and Amos were reconciled, and he returned to England and became a Falcon again. Actually I think that was bound to happen. In his heart he was always a chip off the old block. Those two years being free and easy were fun, but it was never going to last.'

'They might have done. Perhaps something happened to send that side of him into hiding.'

'Kill it off for good, more like,' Freya said robustly. 'Marcel is Amos's son through and through—hard, implacable, money-minded. Will it pay? What will I get out of it, and how can I squeeze more? That's how his mind works.'

'You don't like him, do you?'

'He's all right, always pleasant to me, but Amos can forget about me marrying him. I'd sooner marry the devil.'

'I'm surprised he isn't married already. Rich men don't tend to be short of women.'

'Oh, he's never been short of women,' Freya agreed. 'Just not the kind he's likely to marry, if you see what I mean. They serve their purpose, he pays them off. I believe his 'leaving tips' are quite generous. But he doesn't fall in love.' She gave a brief laugh. 'Don't take me too seriously. I'm only warning you that he'll be tough to work for. After all, you're not likely to want to marry him, are you?'

'Not if I've got any sense,' she said lightly.

'Right, I must be going, but first I need to take some of Marcel's clothes from the wardrobe. He's sleeping out there on the sofa and he says don't worry, he won't trouble you.'

'He's very kind.'

'He can be. Not always. Now I'm off.'

'Goodbye. And thank you.'

Freya slipped out of the door.

Cassie lay in silence, trying to come to terms with the storm of feeling inside her. It had started when she'd glimpsed him tonight, but now it had a new aspect. The woman who now convulsively clenched and unclenched her hands was no longer lovelorn and yearning, but possessed by a bitter anger.

Marcel had known all the time that he was Amos Falcon's son. And he'd deceived her, pretending to be poor as a joke, because it boosted his pride to think she'd chosen him over rich men. It might have started as an innocent game, but the result had been catastrophic.

If I'd known you had a wealthy, powerful father, I wouldn't have given in to Jake. I'd have gone to Amos Falcon, seeking his protection for you. He could have punished Jake, scared him off, and we'd have been safe. We could have been together all these years, and we lost everything because you had to play silly games with the truth. You stupid...stupid...

She pounded the pillow as though trying to release all the fury in her heart, until at last she lay still, exhausted, shocked by the discovery that she could hate him, while the tears poured down her face.

Finally she slept again, and only then did the door open and a figure stand there in silence, watching the faint light that fell from the hallway onto the bed, just touching the blonde hair that streamed across the pillow.

He moved closer to the bed, where he could see her face, relaxed in sleep and more like the face he had once known. In the first moments of their meeting he'd denied the truth to himself, refusing to admit that the evil witch who'd wrecked his life could possibly have returned.

But a witch didn't die. She rose again to laugh over the destruction she had wrought. With every blank word and silent laugh, every look from her beautiful dead eyes, she taunted him.

A wise man would have refused to recognise her, but he'd never been wise where this woman was concerned. Fate had returned her to him, freeing him to make her suffer as he had suffered. And the man whose motto, learned from a powerful, ruthless father, was 'seize every chance, turn everything to your advantage' would not turn away from this opportunity until he'd made the most of it.

Suddenly the figure on the bed before him changed, becoming not her but himself, long ago, shattered with the pain of broken ribs, half blinded by his own blood, but even more by his own tears, longing every moment to see her approach and comfort him, finally realising that she would never do so.

That was when his heart had died. He'd been glad of it ever since. Life was easier without feelings. The women who could be bought were no trouble. They knew their place, did their duty, counted their reward and departed smiling. In time he might choose a wife by the same set of rules. Friends too tended to be business acquaintances. There were plenty of both men and women, there whenever he wanted them. His life was full.

His life was empty. His heart was empty. Safer that way.

He kept quite still for several long minutes, hardly daring to breathe, before closing the door and retreating, careful that she should never know he'd been there.

She awoke to the knowledge that everything had changed. As she'd told Freya, she seemed to have been several people in the last few hours, without knowing which one was really her. But now she knew.

Cassie.

Somewhere in the depths of sleep the decision had been made. She was Cassie, but a different Cassie, angry, defiant, possessed by only one thought.

Make him pay.

He'd treated her with contempt, concealing his true identity because that had been his idea of fun. He hadn't meant any harm, but his silly joke had resulted in years of pain and suffering for her. Perhaps also for him, but she was in no mood to sympathise.

Freya knocked and entered. 'Just came to say goodbye,' she said. 'Marcel is waiting for you to have breakfast with him.'

She dressed hurriedly, twisted her hair into its usual bun and followed Freya out into the main room. Marcel was standing by the window with another man of about seventy, who turned and regarded her with interest.

'Good morning, Mrs Henshaw,' Marcel said politely. 'I'm glad to see you looking well again. This is my father, Amos Falcon.'

'Glad to meet you,' the old man said, shaking her hand while giving her the searching look she guessed was automatic with him. 'Marcel always chooses the best, so I expect great things of you.'

'Father—' Marcel said quickly.

'He's told me that your expertise is unrivalled,' Amos went on. 'So is your local knowledge, which he'll need.'

Since Cassie had refused the job this might have been expected to annoy her, but things were different now. In the last few hours she'd moved to a level so different that it was like being a new person. So she merely smiled and shook Amos Falcon's hand, replying smoothly, 'I hope he finds that I live up to his expectations.'

A slight frisson in the air told her that she'd taken Marcel by surprise. Whatever he'd expected from her, it wasn't this.

'If you'd care to go and sit at the table,' he said, 'I'll be with you in a minute.'

A maid served her at the table in the large window bay. She drank her coffee absent-mindedly, her attention on Marcel, who was bidding farewell to his father and Freya.

Now she had a better view of him than the night before. The lanky boy had turned into a fine man, not only handsome but with an air of confidence, almost haughtiness, that was to be expected from a member of the great Falcon dynasty.

But then haughtiness fell away and he smiled at Freya, bidding her goodbye and taking her into a friendly hug. Cassie noticed that, despite her avowed disdain for him, Freya embraced him cheerfully, while Amos stood back and regarded them with the air of a man calculating the odds.

So it was true what Freya had said. If Amos couldn't marry her to his eldest son, then Marcel was next in line. Doubtless she would bring a substantial dowry for which he could find good use.

Then it was over, they were gone and he was turning back into the room, joining her at the table.

'I owe you my thanks,' he said, 'for not making a fool of me before my father. If you'd told him of your intention to refuse the job I offered I would have looked absurd. I'm grateful to you for your restraint.'

'I doubt it's in my power to make you look absurd,' she said lightly. 'I'm sure you're well armoured against anything I could dream up.'

'Now you're making fun of me. Very well, perhaps I've earned it.'

'You must admit you left yourself rather exposed by allowing your father to think I'd already agreed. Still, I dare say that's a useful method of—shall we say—proceeding without hindrance?'

'It's worked in the past,' he conceded. 'But you're right, it can leave me vulnerable if someone decides to be difficult.' He saw her lips twitching. 'Have I said something funny?'

'How would you define "difficult"? No, on second thoughts don't say. I think I can guess. Someone who dares to hold onto their own opinion instead of meekly obeying you.' She struck an attitude. 'I wonder how I knew that.'

'Possibly because you're much the same?' he suggested.

'Certainly not. I'm far more subtle. But I don't suppose you need to bother with subtlety.'

'Not often,' he agreed, 'although I flatter myself I can manage it when the occasion demands.'

'Well, there's no demand for it now. Plain speaking will suit us both better, so I'll say straight out that I've decided it would suit me to work for you, on certain conditions.'

'The conditions being?'

'Double the salary I'm earning now, as we discussed.'

'And how much is that?'

She gave him the figure. It was a high one, but he seemed untroubled.

'It's a deal. Shake.'

She took the hand he held out to her, bracing herself for the feel of his flesh against hers. Even so, it took all her control not to react to the warmth of his skin. So much had changed, but not this. After ten years it was still the hand that had touched her reverently, then skilfully and with fierce joy. The sensation was so intense that she almost cried out.

From him there was no reaction.

'I'm glad we're agreed on that,' he said calmly. 'Now you can go and give in your notice. Be back here as soon as possible. Before you leave, we'd better exchange information. Email, cellphones.'

She gave him her cellphone number, but he said, 'And the other one.'

'What other one?'

'You've given me the number you give to everyone. Now I want the one you give to only a privileged few.'

'And what about your "privileged" number?'

He wrote it down and handed it to her. 'Now yours.'

She shook her head. 'I don't have one.'

'Mrs Henshaw—'

'It's the truth. I only need one number.'

Now, she realised, he could guess at the emptiness of her life, with no need for a 'privileged' number because there was nobody to give it to. But all he said was, 'You might have told me that before I gave you mine.'

'Then you wouldn't have given it to me. But if you object, here—take it back.'

She held out the paper but he shook his head.

'No point. You could have memorised it by now. Very clever, Mrs Henshaw. I can see I shall have to be careful.'

'If you're having doubts you can always refuse to employ me.'

His eyes met hers and she drew a sharp breath, for there was a gleam in their depths that she hadn't seen before—not for many years. It teased and enticed, challenged, lured her on to danger.

'I'm not going to accept that offer,' he said softly.

She nodded, but before she could speak he added significantly, 'And you know I'm not.'

It could have been no more than courtesy but there was a new note in his voice, an odd note, that made her tense. She was at a crossroads. If she admitted that she did actually know what he meant, the road ahead was a wilderness of confusion.

Ignore the challenge, said the warning voice in her head. Escape while you can.

'How could I know that?' she murmured. 'I don't know you.'

'I think we both know—all that we need to know. The decision has been taken.'

She wanted to cry out. He seemed to be saying that he really had recognised her, that the two of them still lived in a world that excluded the rest of the universe and only they understood the language they spoke.

But no! She wouldn't let herself believe it. She *must not* believe it, lest she go crazy.

Crazier than she'd been for the last ten years? Or was she already beyond hope? She drew a deep breath.

But then, while she was still spinning, he returned to earth with devastating suddenness.

'Now that we've settled that, tell me how you got here last night,' he said.

His voice sounded normal again. They were back to practical matters.

'In a taxi,' she said.

'I'm glad. It's better if you don't drive for a while after what happened.'

'My head's fine. It was only a tiny bump. But I'll take a taxi to the office.'

'Good. I'll call you later. Now I must go. I have an appointment with the bank. We'll meet tomorrow.'

He was gone.

At the office Mr Smith greeted her news with pleasure. When she'd cleared her desk he took her for a final lunch. Over the wine he became expansive.

'It can be a good job as long as you know to be careful. Men like him resemble lions hovering for the kill. Just be sure you're not the prey. Remember that however well he seems to treat you now, all he cares about is making the best use of you. When your usefulness is over you'll be out on your ear. So get what you can out of him before he dumps you.'

'Perhaps he won't,' she said, trying to speak lightly.

'He always does. People serve their purpose, then they're out in the cold. He's known for it.'

'Perhaps there's a reason,' she said quietly. 'Maybe someone deserted him.'

'Don't make me laugh! Dump him? Nobody would dare.'

'Not now perhaps, but in the past, maybe when he was vulnerable—'

Mr Smith's response was a guffaw. 'Him? Vulnerable?

Never. Amos Falcon's son was born fully formed and the image of his father. Hard. Armoured. Unfeeling. Oh, it's not how he comes across at first. He's good with the French fantasy lover stuff. Or so I've heard from some lady friends who were taken in when they should have known better. But don't believe it. It's all on the outside. Inside—nothing!'

'Thanks for the lunch,' she said hurriedly. 'I must be going.'

'Yes, you belong to him now, don't you?'

'My *time* belongs to him,' she corrected. 'Only my time.'

She fled, desperate to get away from the picture he showed her of Marcel—a man damaged beyond hope. Hearing him condemned so glibly made her want to scream.

You don't know him, don't know what he suffered. I knew him when he was generous and loving, with a heart that overflowed, to me at least. He was young and defenceless then, whatever you think.

Only a few hours ago her anger had been directed at Marcel, but now she knew a surge of protective fury that made her want to stand between him and the world. What did any of them understand when nobody knew him as she did?

She checked that her cellphone was switched on and waited for his call. It didn't come. She tried not to feel disappointed, guessing that the bank would occupy him for a long time. And she had something else in mind, for which she would need time to herself.

When she reached home she locked the front door behind her. For the next few hours nothing and nobody must disturb her.

Switching on her computer, she went online and settled down to an evening of research.

She forced herself to be patient, first studying Amos Falcon, which was easy because there were a dozen sites devoted to him. An online encyclopaedia described his life and career—the rise from poverty, the enormous gains in power and money. There was less detail about his private life beyond the fact that he'd had three wives and five sons.

As well as Darius and Marcel there was Jackson Falcon, a minor celebrity in nature broadcasting. Finding his picture, she realised that she'd seen him in several television programmes. Even better known was Travis Falcon, a television actor in America, star of a series just beginning to be shown in England. The last son was Leonid, born and raised in Russia and still living there. About him the encyclopaedia had little information, not even a picture.

There were various business sites analysing Amos's importance in the financial world, and a few ill-natured ones written in a spirit of 'set the record straight'. He was too successful to be popular, and his enemies vented their feelings while being careful to stay just the right side of libel.

The information about Marcel told her little that she hadn't already learned from Freya, but there was much about La Couronne, his hotel in Paris. From here she went to the hotel's own site, then several sites that gave customers' opinions. Mrs Henshaw studied these closely, making detailed notes.

Then Cassie took over, calling up photographs of Marcel that went back several years. Few of them were close-ups. Most had been taken at a distance, as though he was a reluctant subject who could only be caught by chance.

But then she came across a picture that made her grow tense. The date showed that it had been taken nine years ago, yet the change in him was already there. Shocked, she realised that the sternness in his face, the heaviness in his attitude, had settled over him within a year of their separation. This was what misery had done to him.

She reached out and touched the screen as though trying to reach him, turn time back and restore him to the vibrant, loving boy he'd once been. But that could never happen. She snatched her hand back, reminding herself how much of the tragedy was his own fault for concealing the truth. She must cling to that thought or go mad.

She came offline. But, as if driven by some will of their own, her fingers lingered over the keys, bringing up another picture, kept in a secret file. There they were, Cassie and Marcel, locked in each other's embrace. She had many such shots, taken on a delayed release camera borrowed from a photographer friend.

'I want lots of pictures,' she'd told Marcel, 'then we'll always have them to remember this time when we were so happy.'

'I won't need help to remember you,' he'd told her fervently. 'You'll always live in my heart and my memory as you are now, my beautiful Cassie. When I'm old and grey you'll still be there with me, always—always—'

Gently he'd removed her clothes.

'This is my one chance to have a picture of you naked, because I couldn't bear to have any other photographer take them. Nobody else must ever see you like this—only me. Promise me.'

'I promise.'

'Swear it. Swear by Cupid and his bow.'

'I swear by Cupid, his bow and all his arrows.'

As she spoke she was undressing him until they were both naked, and he took her into his arms, turning her towards the clicking camera so that her magnificent breasts could be seen in all their glory.

'This is how I'll always see you,' he murmured. 'When we're old and grey, I'll show you these to remind you that in my heart this is what you really look like.'

'You'll have forgotten me by then,' she teased.

To her surprise, he'd made a sound of anger. 'Why do you say things like that? Don't you know that we must always be together because I will never let you go?'

'I don't want you to let me go.'

But he hardly seemed to hear her.

'Why can't you understand how serious I am? There is only you. There will only ever be you. I'll never let you go, Cassie. Even if there were miles between us I would still be there, holding onto you, refusing to let you forget me. You might try to escape but you won't be able to.'

What mysterious insight had made him utter those words, so strangely prophetic of what was to come? Miles and years had stretched between them, yet always he'd been there as he'd promised—or was it threatened?—always on the edge of her consciousness until the day he'd appeared again to reclaim her.

There it was again, the tormenting question. Had he recognised her, or had she only imagined that he'd called her Cassie?

And his remark that the decision had already been taken, had she not simply read too much into it? Was she hearing what she wanted to hear?

But there was more. Just before she'd left him that morning there had been another clue, if only she could remember what it was. She'd barely noticed at the time, but now she realised that his words had been significant. If only—

Frantically she wracked her memory. It was connected with the cellphone number—something he'd said—something—something—

'What?' she cried out. *'What was it?'*

She dropped her head, resting it on one hand while she slammed the other hand on the table again and again with increasing desperation.

* * *

A few miles away someone else was conjuring up pictures online. The one word, 'Cassie' brought her before him in a website that analysed the careers of models who were no longer around.

For two years she rode high and could have ridden higher still, but suddenly she gave up modelling and disappeared from sight. After that she was occasionally seen in luxurious surroundings, places where only rich men gather. And always she seemed weighed down with diamonds.

Why hadn't he seen it happening? Her choice of himself over wealthy admirers had made him love her a million times more, but it had always been too good to be true. It was a game she'd played, until she'd succumbed to the lure of serious money. While he'd thought he was her true love, he'd been no more than her plaything.

He should have known when she'd failed to visit him in the hospital. He'd lain there in pain and anguish, certain that she would be here at any moment. Every time the door opened he'd tensed with longing, which was always crushed.

He'd clung to the fragile hope that she didn't know what had happened to him. If only he could reach her, all would be well. But her cellphone was switched off. When he'd called her apartment the phone rang and rang, but was never answered.

He'd known then, known with such certainty that he'd torn up the letter she'd sent him without even opening it. Who needed to read her miserable excuses?

He'd seen her just once more, the day he'd left for Paris. There she'd been at the airport with her new lover, as he went into the departure lounge.

'You!' he'd spat. 'The last person I ever want to see.'

She'd held out her arms, crying frantically, 'Marcel, you don't understand—please—please—'

'I loved you,' he raged. 'I trusted you—now I can't bear the sight of you!'

'Marcel—'

'Get out of my sight! *Whore!*'

He'd turned and ran from her. He remembered that afterwards with self-disgust. It was he who had run, not her.

But there would be no running now.

The time had come.

CHAPTER FOUR

WHEN she rose next morning her mind was firm and decided. Today she would start working for Marcel, getting close to the man he'd become, watching to see where the path led. And, wherever it led, she was ready to explore.

Now she was glad that his younger ghost haunted her. Far from trying to banish that spectre, she would enlist him onside and make use of his insights to confront the present man.

She made coffee and toast and sat eating it by the window, looking down at the street, thinking of another time, another window where she'd watched for a grocery delivery. Cassie had been riding high, with two great modelling jobs behind her and more in the offing. The world was wonderful.

And then the most wonderful thing of all had happened.

The grocery van had drawn up and the delivery man stepped out. That was her first view of Marcel's tall, vigorous body. Being only one floor up, she could appreciate every detail. When he'd glanced up she'd seen not only his good looks but the cheeky devil lurking in his eyes. That had been what really won her heart.

It was the same with him. She knew that by the way he came to a sudden halt, as though something had seized him, smiling at her with pleasure and an air of discovery. The words, *That's it! This is the one!* had sung in the air between them.

A week later, lying in each other's arms, he'd said, 'I knew then that I was going to love you.'

'I knew I'd love you too,' she'd assured him joyfully.

'Really? Me, the grocer's delivery lad? With all the men you could have?'

'If I can have them I can also reject them,' she'd pointed out. 'I choose the man I want. *I* choose.' With mock sternness she'd added, 'Don't forget that.'

'No, ma'am. Whatever you say, ma'am.'

He'd given her a comical salute and they'd dissolved into laughter, snuggling down deeper into the bed, and then not laughing at all.

How handsome he'd been that first day, getting out of the van and approaching her. How young, untouched by life!

'Good morning!'

She jumped, startled by the voice that came from below. A car had stopped and a man was calling up to her, pulling her back to the present, where she didn't want to be.

'I'm sorry…who…?'

'I said good morning,' Marcel repeated.

'Oh—it's you!'

'Who were you expecting?'

'Nobody. I thought you'd call me.'

'May I come up?'

'Of course.' She tossed down the keys.

She hadn't dressed and was suddenly conscious of the thin nightie. By the time he arrived she'd pulled on a house coat. It was unflattering, but it zipped up to the neck and at least he wouldn't think she was trying to be seductive. Anything but that.

When she emerged from the bedroom he was already there.

'I'm sorry to arrive so early, but I'm eager to get a close inspection of my new property.'

'Meaning me?' she asked, her head on one side and a satirical smile on her lips.

'A shrewd businesswoman like you should appreciate the description. So I came to collect you, which was perhaps a little thoughtless of me. Finish your breakfast.'

She fetched a cup and poured him a coffee. 'Let's talk. I can eat and work at the same time.'

'I see I've hired the right person. The hotel needs development, the sooner the better.'

'You spoke of making it like La Couronne, and there are several avenues that it would be profitable to explore. The success of your Paris hotel may be because of all the—' She launched into a list gleaned from her investigation of the hotel's website, adding, 'You could probably do some of these things more easily without the problems that arose in—' Here she made use of knowledge found on a business site that spilled the beans about some interesting battles.

'That man who caused you all the trouble didn't really give up, did he?' she asked. 'I gather he's still complaining about—'

Marcel listened to her with raised eyebrows. She could tell that he was impressed. Good. That was how she wanted him. She was taking charge.

'People who come to the London hotel should sense the connection with Paris,' she added. 'It'll be useful when you're ready to expand further.'

'That's looking rather far ahead.'

'But it's what you need to do. Eventually your hotels will be all over Europe, with your trademark. This one could be The Crown Hotel, and the one you'll open in Italy can be La Corona. Spain as well. Then it'll be Die Krone in Germany, De Kroon in Holland. Czech and Slovak will probably have to wait a while—'

'You don't say!' he exclaimed with a grin of wry appreciation.

'But when their time comes it'll be Koruna.'

'You've got this all worked out. And I thought *I* was organised.'

'I like to be prepared. Aren't I supposed to be?'

'Yes, indeed.' He added wryly, 'But how often are people what they're supposed to be?'

'People, rarely. But places can be exactly as planned, if you tackle the problem properly'

'Quite right.' He raised his coffee cup in her direction. 'And with your help that's what will happen.'

She clinked her cup against his. 'Now I must dash and get ready.'

When she'd gone Marcel looked around the apartment, surprised to find it so small and plain. Her fortunes might have dived over the years but a woman in her present position surely didn't need to live among second-hand furniture and walls that looked as though they needed repapering.

From the bathroom he could hear the sound of the shower, which made it awkward that the phone should ring at that moment. Since there was no way he could interrupt her now, he lifted the receiver.

'Is Jane there?' came a man's voice.

'She's occupied right now. Can I say who called?'

'Tell her it's Dave, and I need to talk to her quickly.'

The line went dead.

He replaced the receiver, frowning.

She emerged a few minutes later, fully dressed and with her hair swept back.

'Dave wants you to call him,' Marcel told her. 'It sounded urgent.'

She had seized the receiver before he even finished speaking, leaving him wondering even more curiously about Dave and the hold he evidently had over her.

He tried not to eavesdrop, or so he told himself, but certain phrases couldn't be shut out.

'Dave, it's all right, I'll take care of it. I can't talk now. I'll call you back later.' She hung up.

Marcel didn't speak. He wondered if he was being fanciful in imagining that she had ended the conversation quickly because he was there.

His mind went back years, to their time together. When had she ever spoken to himself in that placating tone? Never.

So what did this man have to make her subservient? Vast wealth?

No, she didn't live like a women with a rich admirer.

Good looks? Other attractions? Could his personal 'skills' make her cry out for more?

'Perhaps it's time we were going,' he said heavily.

She turned to him and her expression was as efficiently cheerful as a mask.

'Tell me something first,' she said briskly. 'Are they expecting you at the Alton?'

'No, I think I'll see more if I take them by surprise.'

'You'll see more if you take a room incognito. But I expect they'd recognise you, so it probably wouldn't work.'

'I doubt if anyone would know me. Are you serious?'

'You said you wanted to take them by surprise. There's no better way than this.'

'I suppose not,' he said slowly. 'I wonder—'

'Leave it to me.' She went to the phone and dialled the Alton's number.

'Hello, do you have a room free today? You do? Excellent. What kind of price? All prices? Really. Run them past me, single rooms and suites.'

As they were given to her, she recited them aloud, watching Marcel's expression of wry understanding. The Alton wasn't doing fantastic business.

'I'll take the best available suite,' he said quietly.

'What name?'

'My real name. I won't have anyone saying I deceived them.'

'Mr Marcel Falcon,' she said into the phone. 'He'll be there today.' She hung up.

He gave her a glance of grim appreciation. 'You're a wicked woman, Mrs Henshaw—I'm glad to say.'

'It has its uses,' she observed lightly.

'So I'll return to the Gloriana to check out. You'd better come with me, then we'll go on to the Alton. I'll wait for you downstairs.'

Once down in the street he glanced up at her window but there was no sign of her. He knew exactly what she was doing— calling Dave now that they could talk privately.

Whoever Dave was!

In this he was wrong. Cassie didn't return Dave's call immediately because there was no need. She knew what he wanted. Instead she went online, gave some instructions, shut the computer down and sent him a text saying, *All taken care of.*

Then she pushed Dave aside. Only Marcel occupied her thoughts now.

Against all reason, she was certain that he recognised her, but only against his will. And he refused to admit it to her.

But he could never deny it to himself. Instinct told her that. Try as he might, Marcel was fighting with Marcel, and it would be a losing battle on both sides.

That told her all she needed to know.

'Right,' she said to Mrs Henshaw in the mirror. 'Let's see if we can give him a run for his money.' She smiled. 'And maybe—just maybe—he'll give me a run for mine. That could be—interesting.'

She could almost have sworn Mrs Henshaw nodded.

The Alton Hotel had a disconsolate air.

'It used to be the London home of a duke,' she observed as they drew up in the car park, 'which is why it was built on such grand lines, but he had to sell it off, and the developers who bought it couldn't afford to complete their plans.'

Checking in went without a hitch. Nobody recognised Marcel and they were able to proceed upstairs to a luxurious suite of four rooms, one of which was dominated by a huge double bed.

Cassie ignored it and went to look out of the window, saying eagerly, 'Just the view I was hoping for. Look at that building next door. It's the one you need to buy to expand this place.'

'Let me see.' He came to stand beside her. 'Yes, it's ideal. I can connect the two and this side will be—'

He talked for a few more minutes but she barely heard him. Her whole body seemed to be hypnotised by the sensation of standing close to him so that the air between them seemed to sing. His extra height loomed over her in a way she'd once loved, and when he casually laid a hand on her shoulder she had to fight not to jump.

'Why don't we go and take a look?' she said.

'I can see all I want from here. I'm going to tear it down, and that's it.'

'I can put you in touch with three excellent building contractors—'

'Can't we just hire the best?'

'With three you can play them off against each other,' she pointed out.

'Splendid. I see you believe in reading your employer's mind and following his instructions exactly.'

'What else am I here for?'

'Then here's another instruction for you. I'll have no grim and forbidding ladies working for me.'

'Are you firing me?' she asked lightly.

'No, I'm telling you to make yourself less severe.'

'Flaunt myself, you mean?' she demanded in a voice that managed to sound shocked. 'Mr Falcon, I hope I've misunderstood you.'

'Only because you're determined to,' he replied with a smile that nearly destroyed her composure. 'I'm going to need you with me a lot of the time—'

'And you think I'm so ugly I'll frighten the horses?' she managed to say lightly.

'You're not ugly. But for some reason you're determined to pretend you are. Now that *is* frightening.'

'Why would any woman want to pretend that?' she murmured.

'A good question. We might talk about it later. Ah, I hear someone at the door. It must be the waiter with my order.'

He moved away and she clutched the windowsill to stop herself swaying. She was trembling from the feel of his hand on her shoulder, and also from the sensation that he too had been trembling.

It took several hours to walk slowly through the building, making notes, trying to be inconspicuous. They ended up back in his suite, thankfully drinking coffee.

'I'll just check my mail,' he said, opening his laptop, which he'd already connected to the hotel's Internet.

He didn't take long, sending a few messages and making a gesture of dismissal.

'Time to think of having some dinner,' he said. 'There's a place upstairs—'

Her phone rang. Marcel watched her face as she answered, saw her expression drop and heard her sigh.

'Dave, I've done my best—'

Dave, he thought. A man with some kind of hold over her, perhaps a man who'd once inspired her love and for whom she still felt some sympathy. Or was he blackmailing her?

'All right, all right,' she was saying. 'I'll send some more. Bye for now.' She turned to Marcel. 'Can I use your computer?'

'Be my guest.'

She was online in a moment, accessing her bank account. Marcel had the impression that she'd forgotten his existence. Totally absorbed, she was trying to transfer a large amount out of her account, into another one. But only trying. The bank refused, saying it would take her over her limit.

'Oh, no!' she said frantically.

'Look, I don't want to pry, but if this man is extorting money from you, then you need help,' Marcel told her.

She looked up as if wondering why he was there.

'Extorting—?'

'Why are you giving him money? Especially money that you clearly can't afford.'

'Dave's married to my sister Laura. They have a lot of financial problems, and I try to help them out.'

'He's…your brother-in-law?' he echoed, astounded.

'Yes, why do you sound so disbelieving?'

He couldn't have told her. It would take time to come to terms with the thoughts whirling chaotically in his head. All he knew was that somewhere the sun had come out.

'He didn't sound like a brother-in-law,' he said lamely.

'I know. He sounds like a needy child because that's what he is,' she said grimly. 'Also they have a little girl who needs a lot of care, so Laura can't take a job. Now, if you'd just give me a moment—'

'Well, I won't. Move over.'

She was forced to yield and let him get to the computer, where he accessed his own bank account in Paris, ordering them to transfer a sum of money to her.

'You'll have to fill in the details of your account,' he said.

She did so, too bewildered to argue, and in a moment it was done.

'Now, you just give the money to Dave and it's finished,' Marcel said.

'Actually, I give it to Laura. That way the bills get paid. He'd just be off down the pub.'

The contempt in her voice was plain. With more relief than he cared to admit, Marcel realised that Dave didn't have the place in her life that he'd suspected.

Dreaded?

'Thank you,' she said as she completed the transaction. 'I don't know how to—'

'Let's be clear. I've come to your aid for entirely selfish reasons. I want your whole attention and I won't get it if you're worried about money.'

'But you gave me so much.'

'Three months' wages in advance. Now you'll have to work for me whether you want to or not.'

'I've already said I will.'

'Yes, but you might have changed your mind.' His lips twisted. 'It's my opinion that women are notoriously unreliable about sticking to their word. So I've taken you prisoner. I'm sorry if you object.'

'I don't. I'm grateful. Laura needs all the help she can get.'

'By help you mean cash. Is that why you live in that shabby little dump?'

'What would you expect? Should I be revelling in the lap of luxury?'

It took him a moment to reply and she had the satisfying feeling that she'd caught him off-guard.

'I wouldn't know, would I?' he asked at last.

'No,' she said quietly. 'How could you?'

'I think we both need a good stiff drink and a large meal,' he said. 'The best restaurant seems to be the one on the roof, and so let's head up there.'

The restaurant had two halves, one with a glass roof, one with no roof at all. As the weather was clement they settled here with a magnificent view over London. In the distance the setting sun blazed crimson as it drifted slowly down the sky.

'It's like watching a fire that you don't have to be afraid of,' she said in wonder.

'Is there such a thing as a fire you need not fear?' he asked.

He spoke lightly, even casually, but she thought she sensed tension beneath the tone.

Only because you're listening for it, said her inner voice sternly. *Be careful of getting paranoid.*

'What did you say?' Marcel asked.

'Nothing, I—'

'It sounded like, "Sometimes paranoid is best."'

'Nonsense.' She laughed edgily. 'I didn't say anything.'

'I thought you did. Ah, here's the waiter. Time for a celebratory supper.'

He ordered the best of everything, including champagne and caviar, seeking her opinion, deferring to her as if she were a queen.

Until your usefulness is ended, Smith reminded her in her mind.

Get lost! she told him.

'What's so amusing?' Marcel asked, looking at her curiously. 'You suddenly started to smile in a very mysterious way. Share the joke.'

'I can't.'

'Ah, a private joke. They're often the most interesting.'

'Only while they stay private.'

'I see. All right, I'll back off—for the moment.'

Suddenly she came to a resolution. Clenching her hands beneath the table where he couldn't see, she said, 'There's something I meant to ask you,' she said.

'Go on.'

'When I fell against the tree, I thought I heard you call me Cassie. Who is she?'

He didn't reply at once, only looked at her strangely, as though trying to make up his mind. With sudden devastating insight she saw herself through his eyes—the severe clothes, the flattened hair, the steel-rimmed spectacles. She could even hear his thoughts. *How could I ever have thought this was her?*

'Just a girl I once knew,' he said at last.

'And you confused me with her? Am I like her?'

'Not at all,' he said instantly. 'The way she looked, the way she dressed—she gave herself to the world, at least—'

'Yes?' she urged when he didn't go on.

'Nothing.'

'She gave herself to the world, meaning I don't?'

'I think you prefer to withdraw and hide deep inside yourself.'

She laughed. 'That's one way of putting it. You said I looked grim and forbidding, and recently someone said I looked like a prison wardress.'

'To your face?'

'No, he didn't realise that I could hear.'

'You sound remarkably cheerful about it. Most women would be hurt or offended.'

'I'm not most women.'

'Indeed you're not. I'm beginning to understand that.'

'In my job it's an advantage if people think I'm dreary. They ignore me and overlook me, which is useful. You learn a lot when people have forgotten you're there.'

'But you're not at work every hour. What about the rest of the time?'

She gave a carefully calculated shrug. 'What rest of the time? Life is work, making a profit, turning everything to your advantage. What else?'

'You say that but you don't live by it, otherwise you wouldn't let your family bleed you dry.'

She shrugged. 'Their needs just mean that I have to make twice as much profit, be twice as determined to manage life my way. Eventually I'll make so much money that I can afford to help them *and* become a financial tyrant.'

'It has to be a tyrant, does it?'

'They seem to be the kind that flourish best.'

'Some people think there are other things that matter.' He was watching her.

'Some people are losers,' she observed.

'They certainly are,' he said slowly. 'No doubt about that. But not us. That's true, isn't it?'

'That's definitely true.'

The champagne arrived. Marcel filled both glasses and raised his. 'I think we should toast ourselves. To us and what we're going to achieve.' They clinked.

'I'm looking forward to the moment when you see La Couronne.'

'Am I going to?'

'Yes, I think we should head there as soon as possible. My lawyer here can deal with the formalities. When you've seen what there is in Paris you'll be better placed to take charge in London.'

'I must warn you that my French is very poor.'

'Really? I thought such an efficient lady must be an expert.'

'I know a few words—very limited—'

Mon seul amour, je t'aime pour toujours—

Words of passionate adoration that she had learned from him, and repeated with all her heart. To please him, as a surprise, she'd started to learn the language properly, but their parting had come before she could tell him.

'Don't worry,' he said now. 'There are so many English tourists in Paris that I insist that all my employees speak the language.'

'How long will I need to be in Paris?'

'Several weeks at least. Is that a problem?'

'No, but I shall need to sort out my affairs here. Perhaps I can take tomorrow off to make my arrangements.'

'Very well. Do you have other relatives? I assume you have no children since your sister and her family take so much from you. But what about Mr Henshaw? Does he have no claims?'

'None,' she said shortly. She held out her glass. 'Can I have another champagne?'

When Marcel had filled her glass she rose and went to the edge of the roof, leaning on the wall and looking down at London, where the lights had come on, glimmering in the darkness.

Mr Henshaw had never existed, although there had been a husband, one who still haunted her nightmares. She tried never to think of him and mostly succeeded, with that inner control that had become her most notable characteristic. But now events had brought him back so that he seemed to be there, infusing the air about her with fear and horror.

And there was no escape.

CHAPTER FIVE

LIFE with Jake had been a nightmare. He'd set his heart on marrying her and pestered her morning, noon and night. She'd refused, clinging to the hope that Marcel would come looking for her. Even after the agony of their last meeting she thought it might happen. He would suffer, lying in the darkness for long, sleepless nights, and during those nights the memories would come back to him. He would relive the joy of their youthful love, and at last he would realise that such love could never end in the way that theirs had seemed to. Then he would search for her, rescue her, and they would be together again.

But it hadn't happened. Days had become weeks, weeks passed into months and the silence stretched ahead endlessly. At last she'd faced the truth. Marcel hated her. For him she no longer existed. There would be no reunion, no hope of future happiness.

In this state of despair all energy had seemed to leave her. She no longer had the vigour to fight, and when Jake had marched in one day, seized her hand and slid a magnificent engagement ring onto it, she simply stared and left it there.

After that he was shrewd enough to move fast, arranging the wedding for the soonest possible date and never letting her out of his sight. In only one matter did she find the strength to oppose him, declaring that she would not be married in church. It must be a civil ceremony only. She refused to insult any religious establishment with this mockery of a wedding. Jake didn't care. As long as he claimed her it didn't matter how.

The ring he gave her was a spectacular creation of diamonds and sapphires, clearly designed to be a trophy. It was Jake's proof that he owned her.

The three years of her marriage were strange and haunted. He swore a thousand times that he was madly in love with her, and she came to believe that, in his own way, he was. He was cruel and egotistical, grasping whatever he wanted and careless of whom he hurt. But, like many selfish brutes, he had a sentimental streak. Cassie had a hold on his heart that nobody else could claim, and he took this as proof of his own humanity.

It gave her a kind of power, and she discovered that power could be enjoyable, especially when it was all you had. Jake's eagerness to please her was ironic, but she could use it to make him give money to charity. She supported two particular charities, one for children, one for animals, and for them she extracted as much as she could from Jake.

Afterwards he expected to be repaid. 'Now you'll be nice to me, won't you?' he'd say, and she would yield to the night that followed, trying not to show her revulsion. What Jake called 'love-making' was so horribly different to what she had known with Marcel that it came from another universe, one where she had to endure being slobbered over and violated.

At first she tried to pretend that she was back in the arms of her true love, but the contrast was so cruel that she gave it up in sheer self-defence. Otherwise she would have genuinely gone mad.

It was almost a relief to become pregnant, and have an excuse to banish Jake from her bed. Slightly to her surprise he accepted her decision without argument. At the thought of producing the next generation his sentimental streak was asserting itself again, and he withdrew to protect her.

And now she could at least feel that life held out some hope for her. She would have a child to love, a purpose in life.

But after five months she miscarried. No doctor could tell her why. There had been no accident, no trauma. It had simply happened, leaving her staring into a blank future.

Hope came from an unexpected source. By chance she discovered that Jake had been playing around.

'It's not my fault,' he defended himself. 'It's months since we could…well, it'll be different now.'

'Yes, it's going to be different,' she agreed. 'I'm divorcing you.'

His howls of protest left her unmoved, and so did his threats.

'If you want to destroy me, Jake, go ahead. What do you think is left to destroy? Do your worst. I don't care.'

Perhaps it was the thought of how many of his disreputable secrets she'd learned that warned him to be cautious. But something made him cave in. Before he could change his mind she hurled back at him every expensive gift he'd ever given her, including the engagement ring. Then she moved out the same day.

He made one last attempt to persuade her to remain his wife. When that failed he tried to get her to accept a financial settlement.

She agreed to very little for the sake of her family, but took nothing for herself. 'If I live off your money you'll still think you control me,' she told him. 'And I want to forget that you ever existed.'

He paled. 'You're breaking my heart,' he choked.

And he meant it, she thought afterwards. Oddly enough, this unpleasant man had a heart to break, where she was concerned. But it left her untouched. She no longer feared him. All she felt was a heady sensation of power at having brought him down.

She rejected his name, calling herself Henshaw because it had been her mother's maiden name, and using the 'Mrs' because she thought it made her sound older and more serious.

Refusing to live off Jake's money satisfied her but left her penniless. There was no chance of returning to modelling, even if she'd wanted to. Most people would still have called her beautiful, but she felt her magic 'something' had vanished for ever. She'd taken any menial job she could get, using her free time to go to evening classes, studying business to the point of exhaustion. She'd emerged triumphant, going to work in a bank and climbing fast. She had never looked back.

Now she was near the top of the tree, trying to believe it had all been worth it.

But as she looked back at Marcel, sitting quietly, watching her, she was filled with such a rush of hostility that she could have struck him down and enjoyed doing it.

You could have saved me, she thought. *If I'd known who you really were I'd have appealed to your father, and everything could have been different. Oh, why weren't you honest with me? You could have saved me from Jake, from that terrible marriage, losing my child. You could have stopped me turning into a heartless robot, but when it happened I had nowhere to turn. Damn you!*

'What's the matter?' Marcel asked, rising and coming beside her. 'You look upset.'

'Not at all,' she said brightly. 'I was just enjoying the view and the fresh air.'

'Come away from the ledge.' He led her firmly back to the table and stood over her until she was seated.

'Go on telling me about your life,' he said. 'What happened to your husband? Did you walk out on him?'

Like I did with you, you mean? she thought ironically. *That's what you're thinking right now, although you won't come out and say so.*

'Yes, I left him,' she said. 'But only because he was sleeping with someone else.'

Let's see what you make of that! If you want revenge I've just given it to you. But is that what you want? If only I knew.

'I hope he made some financial provision for you,' Marcel said politely.

'I wouldn't let him. It would have given him a hold on me, and no man has that. Ever.'

'When you finish with a man you really finish with him,' he murmured.

'It's the only way.' She gave a sharp, defiant laugh. 'When I've finished with him, he no longer exists.'

'No looking back?'

'Looking back is scary,' she whispered. 'It fills you with hate and makes you want to do things that you know you shouldn't, so then the person you hate is yourself.'

She didn't look at him as she said it. She didn't dare. And his reply was so soft that another person might have missed it. But she was alive to everything about him, and she heard the quiet words with their ominous warning.

'That's very true.'

She glanced at him just in time to meet his eyes, but not in time to read their expression before he looked away. She waited, hoping that he would turn back to her and they might even find a way to talk. But his eyes were fixed on the distance and the silence between them was as deafening as a roar.

All around them the lights were sparkling, arranged in arches by the walls, with dainty lamps near the tables.

The atmosphere on the roof had changed, grown softer, sentimental. This was a place for romantic trysts, with lovers' eyes meeting over the rims of wine glasses. Here there should be smiles of heartfelt understanding, unspoken promises of love. It was a world apart and anyone who did not belong in that world had no right to be here.

I don't belong, she thought wearily. *I did once. Not any more.*

Nearby was a couple sitting close together. The man was middle-aged and heavy. The girl was about twenty, gorgeous and flaunting it. She might have been the young Cassie.

'I guess there's no point in me trying to talk to him tonight,' said a male voice nearby. 'Sorry,' he added hastily, as Marcel and Cassie turned to look at him. 'It's just that I'd planned to talk business with that fellow.'

Marcel grinned. 'No chance now.'

'We should never have agreed to meet here. Too many good-time girls as a distraction. I gather this place is known for it. Everywhere you look there's a lush female trying to seduce a man into parting from his money.' He seemed to become aware of Cassie and hastily added, 'Forgive me. Not you, of course!'

'Of course,' she said.

'I mean you're obviously a very…sensible…businesslike woman, and I didn't mean to insult you.'

She regarded him with ironic humour. 'You mean it's quite impossible that I could ever lead a man down dark and dangerous paths? Some women would be more insulted by that than the other.'

'Look I…put my foot in it. I apologise.'

He retreated in a flurry of embarrassment.

'Well, you certainly made him sorry,' Marcel declared.

She managed to laugh. 'I did, didn't I? His face!'

The man had gone to join the couple at the other table,

talking wildly and making gestures, clearly explaining something to them. He glanced up, saw Cassie looking at him and gave her an embarrassed grin.

'He's terrified of me,' she murmured to Marcel.

'And you don't mind?'

'Why should I mind? I don't want to lead him down "dark and dangerous paths". Hey, the girl's looking at me now. I wonder if she's taking warning.'

'That your gaze might turn her to stone?' Marcel hazarded hilariously.

'No, that a woman can start out like her and end like me. Not that she'd believe it.'

She had a dizzying sensation of going too far. Surely now Marcel must be remembering the dark and dangerous paths down which they'd travelled together, and reading the truth in her eyes. But the time was not right. If things had been different she could have told him everything now, but that was impossible until he could bring himself to admit that he knew who she was.

And that day might never come.

Suddenly she doubted that she had the strength for this. She wanted to cry aloud and flee him. She even moved to rise from her seat, but his hand detained her.

'Are you all right? You look troubled.'

His voice was gentle, his eyes warm and concerned. It was as though another man had taken him over, or perhaps lured him back to the past, and it was her undoing.

'Look, I must go. It's late and I'm tired—'

'Of course. I'll take you home.'

'No!' The word was almost violent. 'No, there's no need for that. I'll be all right.'

'I'll tell Hotel Reception to send a car to the front for you. Then you'll be free of me.'

'It's not that—' she began wildly.

'Yes, it is,' he said. 'It's like that for both of us.' His voice grew softer, more intense. 'We both need some time to get our heads together.' His eyes met hers. 'Don't we?'

She nodded dumbly.

He escorted her out of the hotel and to the waiting car, assisted her into a seat at the rear, then stood with the door still open, leaning in slightly, holding onto her hand.

'It's all right about going to Paris, isn't it?' he asked.

'Of course.'

'Then be ready to travel tomorrow.'

'Tomorrow? But you said I could have the day off to sort out—'

'I've changed my mind. There's no time. You'll have to do it long-distance when you get there. I'll collect you at nine tomorrow morning.' His hand tightened on hers. 'You will be there, won't you?'

'Of course.'

'You won't vanish?'

'No.'

'Promise me.' His voice was almost harsh in its intensity.

'I promise,' she said.

His eyes held hers and for a moment she thought he would refuse to let go of her hand. But then he released her suddenly, slammed the door and stepped back. Her last view of him was standing there, completely still, his eyes fixed on the retreating car like a man clinging on to a vanishing hope.

He watched her until she was out of sight, then took out his phone and dialled a number given to him by his father. It was a private security firm. In a hard voice he gave her address.

'These are your instructions. You park outside and watch. If she comes out with a suitcase and gets into a taxi you call me. Then follow her. And don't let her out of your sight for a moment.'

* * *

In her time with Jake, Cassie had grown used to his ways of flaunting his wealth and what he fondly believed to be his status. He would book the most expensive seats on planes, then arrive at the last minute with the maximum of fuss.

Marcel, in contrast, reached the airport early, got through the formalities with courtesy and was driven quietly to the private jet that was waiting for him.

'My father's,' he explained.

The plane was pure luxury. It could seat eight people in soft, comfortable seats, and had its own galley from which food and drink was served to the two of them by a steward who existed solely for their comfort.

As they began to move down the runway he said, 'The weather's fine so it should be a smooth flight. Nothing to worry about.'

So he remembered that she was afraid of flying, she thought. After one modelling job she'd returned home still shaken and distraught from a bumpy flight. How bright his eyes had been, how full of expectancy for the night of passion to come. And how quickly he'd forgotten all thoughts of his own pleasure to take her trembling body in his arms and soothe her tenderly. There had been no sex that night, and in the morning she had loved him more than ever for his generosity.

'Have you ever been to Paris?' he asked now.

'No, but I've always wanted to. I'm looking forward to exploring it.'

'You won't have time for that. You'll live in the hotel, and have a desk in my office. Everything will be provided to help with your work and you'll be "confined to barracks", forbidden to leave.'

For a moment she almost thought he meant it, but just in time she saw the gleam of wicked humour in his eyes.

'Yeah, right!' she said cynically.

'You don't believe me? Wait until you see the locks on the doors.'

'Nonsense!'

'That's no way to talk to your employer.'

'If you were any other employer I wouldn't, but we both know that I'm not just here to study the facts of La Couronne. I'm here to absorb the atmosphere, and that means the atmosphere of the city as well.'

'Very subtle,' he said appreciatively. 'So you'll arrange the job to suit yourself.'

'It's what I'm good at,' she said impishly. 'Being in control.'

He grinned. She smiled back, happy in this brief moment of warmth and ease between them. But then a scream burst from her as the plane jerked and plunged a few feet.

'Sorry,' came the pilot's voice. 'Air pocket. It's going to be a little turbulent.'

'Don't worry.' Marcel took both her hands in his. 'It'll be over soon. There's no danger.'

'I know it's not dangerous,' she said huskily. 'It's just… being shaken…'

'Just hold onto me.' His hands tightened.

She did so, closing her eyes and shaking her head. It was foolish to be scared but she couldn't help it. As the plane shuddered she whispered, 'No, no, no—'

'Look at me,' Marcel commanded. 'Open your eyes.'

She did so, and the world vanished. His gaze held hers as firmly as if he had her in chains. And they were the most dangerous chains of all because she had no wish to break them.

'It's all right,' he said. 'It's finishing now.'

He was right. The plane's juddering was fading, then ceasing altogether. But that wasn't why the sense of peace and safety was stealing over her. She held him tightly because while he was there nothing could go wrong.

'I'm sorry,' she said in a shaking voice. 'It's stupid to be scared—'

'We all have our nightmares. They don't have to make sense.'

She managed an edgy laugh. 'So much for being in control.'

'We'd all like to be in control,' he said quietly. 'And we all spend our lives discovering how wrong we are.'

'No,' she said defensively. 'I don't believe it has to be like that.'

'I only wish you were right.'

He looked down at their hands, still clasped, and gently released her. She had to suppress the impulse to hold on, refusing to let him go. But she must not give in. She was strong. She was in control. She'd just said so.

At the airport a limousine was waiting to convey them into the heart of Paris. She watched in delight as the landmarks glided past, and they came to a halt in the Champs Elysées in the glamorous heart of the city.

La Couronne towered above her, grandiose and beautiful. Stewards hurried forward to greet their employer and regard herself with curiosity. One of them seized Cassie's bags and invited her to follow him.

'I'll join you later,' Marcel said.

Her accommodation was high up, a luxurious suite where a maid was waiting for her. She'd been wondering what to expect, but the reality took her breath away.

'My name is Tina,' said the maid. 'I am here to serve you. I will start unpacking.'

'Thank you. I'll go and freshen up.'

She went into the bathroom and regarded herself critically in the mirror. Marcel had told her to soften her appearance, but so far she hadn't done so. On the journey he'd glanced at her appearance but made no comment. Now she loosened her hair, letting it fall about her face, not in waves as he'd once known it, but long and straight.

I'm not really Cassie any more, she thought. *I've been fooling myself.*

Sighing in frustration, she left the bathroom and immediately halted at the sight that met her eyes.

'Tina let me in,' Marcel said. 'I came to see how you were settling. If you're ready I'll show you around.'

'Fine, I'm almost finished. I'll just—' She raised a hand to her hair, but he stopped her.

'Leave it.'

'But it's all over the place. I can't go around looking as though I'd been pulled through a hedge backwards.'

'True, but it won't take much to make you a little neater. Just brush it back here—and here—'

As he spoke he was flicking his fingers against her blonde locks, sending them spinning back over her shoulders, then smoothing them away. She tried not to be conscious of his fingertips softly brushing her face, but some things could never be driven away. The touch of a lover's hand, the feel of his breath whispering against her face in agitated waves.

But he's no longer my lover. Remember that.

Firmly she pushed feelings aside. She couldn't afford them.

'Let's go,' she said. 'I really want to see the hotel.'

'I suppose you've read enough to know the background,' he said, showing her outside.

'I know it was once the home of the Marquis de Montpelier, a friend of royalty, who could have anything he wanted, including three wives, five mistresses and more children than he could count.'

'Until the Revolution began, and they all went to the guillotine,' Marcel supplied. 'If you look out of this window you can almost see the place where they died.'

There in the distance she could just make out the Place de la Concorde, where the guillotine had once stood.

'I wonder how often they looked at that view, never dreaming of what would happen to them in the end,' she murmured.

Now, she thought, their palace was the centre of a business empire, and the man who controlled it was safely armoured against all life could do to him.

'Some of the building still looks as it did then,' Marcel told her. 'I keep it that way for the historical interest. Plus I have a friend who claims to have second sight and swears she can see the ghosts of the Montpelier family, carrying their heads under their arms.'

'And you make the most of it,' she said, amused.

'Let's say the rooms on that corridor are always the first to be hired.'

'Do you live on that corridor?'

He grinned. 'No, I don't like to be disturbed by howling spectres.'

As they went over the building she recorded her impressions into a small microphone while Marcel listened, impressed.

'Now let's go to my apartment,' he said, 'unless you're tired.'

'No, let's keep working.'

She was eager to see where he lived and learn what it could tell her about his present personality. But when they arrived she was disappointed. Only the room he used as an office was accessible. The rest was kept hidden behind closed doors.

'I'll be back in a moment,' he said. 'Access anything you want on the computer.'

He went out into the corridor, and she began to familiarise herself with his computer, which was state-of-the-art. She had expected no less. There was a mountain of information for her to take in and she went quickly from one item to the next. A casual onlooker would think she couldn't possibly be absorbing information with such brief glances, but that would be a mistake. She had a photographic memory, which in the old days she'd hidden because it clashed with her sexy image. Marcel had been one of the few people to discover that beneath the ditzy surface was a mind like a machine.

That was it!

She gasped as she realised that she had the answer to the question that had teased her. When she and Marcel had exchanged phone details yesterday, she'd offered to return his and he'd said, 'You could have memorised it by now.'

She'd barely glanced at the scrap of paper, yet he'd known that would be enough for her because he knew something about her that no stranger could have known.

'A great brain', he'd called her, laughing as he clasped her in his arms.

'How do I dare to make love to a woman with such a great brain? A mighty brain! A genius! Some men might find that intimidating.'

'But not you, hmm?'

'No, because she has other virtues. Come here!'

Now, sitting in Marcel's office, she began to shake with the violence of the emotion possessing her. She'd guessed that he recognised her, but now she was sure. He had brought her here, to the heart of his own world. Couldn't she dare to hope that they might open their arms to each other and put right the wrongs of the past?

She'd thought she wanted vengeance, but that was being crowded out by other sensations beyond her control.

Now was the moment, and she would seize it with eager hands. If only he would return quickly.

She heard footsteps in the corridor. He was coming. In just a few moments everything would be transformed. The old attraction was beginning to rise up inside her, and surely it was the same with him. There might even be happiness again.

But the next instant the dream died, smashed to smithereens by something she knew she should have anticipated, but had carelessly overlooked.

Which meant there was no one to blame but herself.

CHAPTER SIX

FROM outside came an urgent tapping on the door and a woman's voice in a high-pitched scream of excitement.

'Marcel, mon chéri—ouvrez le porte et me prendre dans tes bras. Oh, combien je suis heureux que mon véritable amour est de retour.'

Her limited French was just up to translating this.

'Marcel, my darling—open the door and take me in your arms. Oh, how happy I am that my true love has returned.'

So that was that. Another stupid fantasy destroyed.

Don't be so naïve again!

Bringing herself under control, she opened the door and backed away just in time to avoid being lovingly throttled by a girl who was young, sexy, beautiful, vibrant with life.

And she'd called Marcel 'my true love'.

The newcomer began to babble again in French, then switched abruptly to English.

'I'm sorry—you must be Mrs Henshaw—and English, yes?'

'Yes.'

'Marcel has told us all about you.'

'Us?'

'My papa is Raul Lenoir, Marcel's lawyer. He has spoken much of Mrs Henshaw, his new assistant who will handle important business for him in London. I am so pleased to meet you.'

Cassie took the hand she held out, murmuring untruthfully, 'And I am pleased to meet you.'

'My name is Brigitte Lenoir. Where is Marcel? I have missed him so much.'

'He went out a moment ago, but he'll be back soon.'

'Oh I can't wait. I have so much to tell him.'

'I think that's him now.'

The door opened and Marcel appeared, his face brightening as he saw his visitor. They next moment they were in each other's arms. Brigitte covered his face with kisses and he laughed, returning the compliment again and again.

'Brigitte, *ma chérie, mon amante*—'

Cassie returned to the computer, trying not to hear the sounds coming from behind her.

'Brigitte, I want you to meet Mrs Henshaw,' Marcel said at last, freeing himself from her clasp.

'But we have already met, and I am so impressed,' Brigitte declared.

'So you should be,' Marcel said. 'She's a great brain and we're all afraid of her.'

'Papa will be most interested to meet her. You must both come to dinner with us tonight.'

Cassie flinched. 'I'm not sure—'

'Oh, but you must,' Brigitte assured her.

Both her mind and heart rebelled at the thought of spending an evening with these two, watching them all over each other.

'I have a lot of work to do—'

Brigitte began to mutter in French. Without understanding every word, Cassie gathered that she was telling Marcel that he must persuade her. Another woman was vital and Mrs Henshaw would be useful.

'She's just what we need. She can keep Henri talking without—you know—'

The meaning of 'you know' was all too clear. Whoever Henri was, her duty was to keep him talking without attracting him in a way that might be 'inconvenient'. In other words, a plain woman. Like Mrs Henshaw.

'I applaud your desire to work,' Marcel told her, 'but joining us for dinner tonight will be part of that work. We'll dine in the hotel's most splendid restaurant, and you can give me your opinion of it later. Now, I suggest you return to your suite and prepare for tonight.'

Leaving him free to succumb to Brigitte's charms, she thought. As she walked away down the corridor she could hear shrieks of laughter which abruptly faded into murmurs. She increased her speed.

In her rooms she found Tina just finishing, and complimented her on the job.

'It looks so comfortable in here. If only I could just put my feet up, but I've got to attend a formal dinner tonight, with the lawyer and somebody called Henri. Why? What's up?' Tina had smothered a laugh.

'Forgive me, *madame,* but if Henri Lenoir is there it will not be formal.'

'You know him?'

'He is the son of the lawyer and Mademoiselle Brigitte's brother. But apart from that—' Tina hesitated before going on, 'Every girl knows him. He is a very naughty man. The rumour says that his wife has thrown him out for the third time.'

'Because of—?'

'Because he's naughty with many ladies. They say he's returned to his father's home, and the family is watching over him to make sure that…well…'

'That he isn't naughty again. I see.'

'If he behaves she may take him back.'

And evidently Brigitte saw no danger of her brother mis-behaving with Mrs Henshaw. It was practically an insult.

When Tina had gone she threw herself onto the bed, reliv-ing the scene she had just endured. Something had happened that hurt more than anything else so far.

A great brain!

That was what Marcel had called her to Brigitte, but using the words so differently from the way he had once spoken them to herself that now the tears welled up and she rolled over, burying her face in the pillow. Suddenly there was only despair, with nothing to hope for, and she yielded to the dark-ness, weeping until she was too drained to weep any more.

As she recovered she realised that Marcel hadn't given her details about when, where and how to present herself tonight. Quickly she called his cellphone, but it had been switched off. She tried his hotel phone but it stayed unanswered.

Whatever he was doing left him with no attention for any-thing else.

She stared up at the ceiling, aware that she had reached a crossroads. Since Marcel had reappeared in her life she'd been cautious to the point of dithering.

'Not any more,' she vowed. 'Time for a final decision, and I'm making it.'

When Brigitte had finally departed Marcel paced the floor restlessly.

Today he'd shocked himself by doing things he'd never intended, and not doing things he'd vowed were essential.

He'd brought Cassie here to redress the past, although the meaning of that was still vague in his mind. To let her see the riches she'd thrown away, show her the life she could have had instead of the bleak impoverished existence she had now—yes, definitely.

Revenge? Possibly.

But during the flight there had been an unexpected change. At the first sign that she might be vulnerable he'd known a passionate desire to protect her. It was what he'd felt long ago and she'd thrown it back in his face, yet it had leapt out of the darkness at him, like an animal waiting to pounce. And, weakling that he was, he'd yielded to it.

No more weakness. Bringing her here had been a risk, but he wouldn't back down now. One day soon he would confront her with all the memories she seemed determined to avoid. Then she would answer for what she had done to him.

But that must wait until he was ready.

In one sense at least Cassie and Mrs Henshaw were the same person. When a decision was taken there were no second thoughts, no weakening, only a determined follow-through to the end.

This particular decision took her downstairs on winged feet, heading for the fashion shop at the back of the hotel. After studying several glamorous gowns she rejected them all in favour of a pair of tight black satin trousers. Only a woman with her very slender figure could have worn such a garment, but that suited her just fine. To go with them she bought a black silk top with a plunging neckline and bare arms.

It was outrageous, and for a brief moment she hesitated. But then she recalled Brigitte's face that afternoon, not in the least troubled by the sight of her.

'So you're not afraid of Mrs Henshaw,' she addressed the vision. 'Let's see if Cassie can scare you.' She gave a brief laugh. 'Perhaps she ought to. She's beginning to scare me.'

At the beauty salon she described how she wanted to look, aware of the stares of the assistants, incredulous that this plain Jane could indulge such fantasies. But they smiled and got to

work, and when they'd finished her curled hair was tumbling
over her shoulders, partly—but only partly—hiding her daring décolletage.

Back in her room she inspected the satin trousers, wondering if she was being wise. She had a dress that would do.
It was adequate rather than outstanding, but that might just
be better than outrageous.

She tried on the dress, then removed it and donned the
trousers, fighting temptation as she studied her magnificent
appearance in the mirror.

'Oh, heck!' she sighed at last. 'I can't do it, can I? But one
day I will do it. I must. I can't settle for being "adequate" for
ever, but just for tonight maybe I should.'

There was a knock at the door.

'I'm coming,' she called without opening it. 'Just give me
a moment.'

'No, now,' came Marcel's voice. 'I need to talk to you at
once.'

She opened the door, pulling it back against her and retreating so that she was mostly concealed behind it. Even so,
he could see the cascade of her glorious hair and it stopped
him short.

She could have screamed with frustration. The stunned
look on his face was the one she'd longed to see, but what
maddening fate had made it happen just at this moment?

'Mrs…I don't…I wasn't expecting…' He was stammering,
which would have filled her with delight at any other time.

'You said I should look less severe,' she told him loftily.
'Is this sufficiently "un-severe" for you?'

'I…that wasn't…yes…I suppose…'

The last time she'd seen him lost for words was nine years
ago when her landlady had walked in when they were lying
naked on the floor.

'I'm glad you approve,' she said now, still taking care to

conceal as much of herself as possible. 'Is the Lenoir family here yet?'

'Part of it. Madame Lenoir won't be coming, but there's—'

'Marcel, *ou êtes vous?*' Brigitte's voice came floating down the corridor.

'I'm here, *chérie.*'

She was speaking French in a low voice, clearly meaning not to be overheard. Even so, Cassie managed to make out enough to learn that the mysterious Henri was reluctant to attend the dinner, not wanting to be saddled with 'the English woman nobody else wanted'. He'd agreed only on condition that he could leave early. Marcel gave a sharp intake of breath, but could say no more because of sounds from further along the corridor. Two men were approaching, hailing them, receiving Marcel's greeting in return. Then they were in the room, full of polite bonhomie.

'We can't wait to meet the brilliant lady you've brought with you,' Monsieur Lenoir declared. 'Isn't that so, Henri?'

'I've been looking forward to this moment all day,' came a courteous if unconvincing voice. 'Where is she?'

'Here,' Cassie said, stepping out from behind the door.

With the first glance Cassie understood everything she'd heard about Henri. Good looking in a 'pretty boy' style, he had a self-indulgent manner and dark hair worn slightly too long for his age, which she guessed at about forty. Definitely a 'naughty man', fighting the years.

His behaviour confirmed it. He was wide-eyed at the vision that confronted him.

'*Madame,*' he murmured, 'I am more glad to meet you than I can say.' He advanced with his hands out. 'What an evening we are going to have!'

He would have thrown his arms around Cassie, but she stopped him by placing her hands in his. Nothing daunted, he kissed the back of each hand. Then he jerked her forward and in this way managed to embrace her. Turning her head against his shoulder, she had a searing vision of Marcel's face as he gained his first complete sight of her.

What she saw would stay with her for ever. For one blinding second he looked like a man struck over the heart—astonished, bewildered, aghast, shattered. But in the next instant it was all gone, and only a stone mask remained.

No matter. She'd seen all that she needed to see. He'd expected to find Mrs Henshaw, but Cassie's ghost had walked and nothing would ever be the same.

Now she was glad there hadn't been time to change into something more respectable. There was a time for restraint and a time for defiance. Mrs Henshaw would have been left floundering, but Cassie was the expert.

Monsieur Lenoir cleared his throat and came forward, sounding embarrassed. 'Madame Henshaw, allow me to introduce my son.'

'Well, I think he's already introduced himself,' Cassie said with a little giggle.

'But you haven't introduced *your*self,' Henri said.

Brigitte intervened. 'Mrs Henshaw is masterminding Marcel's purchase of the London hotel.'

'That's a bit of an exaggeration,' Cassie said hastily. 'I'm not exactly masterminding it.'

'But Marcel says that you are a great brain,' Brigitte reminded her.

'I'm no such thing,' she defended herself.

Henri gave an exaggerated sigh of relief. 'Thank goodness for that. Brainy women terrify me.'

'Then you've nothing to fear from me,' she cooed, giving him her best teasing smile.

'But you must be brainy or Marcel wouldn't have employed you,' Brigitte pointed out.

'That's true,' Cassie said as if suddenly realising. 'I must be brighter than I thought.'

Her eyes met Marcel's, seeing in them floundering confusion wrestling ineffectively with anger. She was beginning to enjoy herself.

'It's time were going,' Monsieur Lenoir declared, edging his son firmly out of the way and offering Cassie his arm. 'Madame Henshaw, may I have the pleasure of escorting you?'

'The pleasure is mine,' she replied.

But then Henri too stepped forward, offering his other arm so that she walked out of the door with a man on each side, leaving Marcel to follow with Brigitte.

They made a glamorous spectacle as they went along the corridor, the men in dinner jackets and bow ties, Brigitte in flowing evening gown, and Cassie in her luxurious black satin that left nothing to the imagination.

Perhaps that was why Marcel never so much as glanced at her as they went down in the elevator.

But as they stepped out and headed for the restaurant he raised his voice. 'Mrs Henshaw, there's a small matter of business we need to clear up before the evening starts. The rest of you go on and we'll join you.'

His hand on her arm was urgent, holding her back and drawing her around a corner, where there was nobody to see them.

'Just what do you think you're doing?' he muttered furiously.

'Being civil to the people who are important to you.'

'You know what I mean—the way you're dressed—'

'But you told me to.'

'I—?'

'Be less severe, you said. And only today you brushed my hair forward so that—'

'Never mind that,' he said hastily.

'I'm only doing what I thought you wanted. Oh, dear!' She gasped as if in shocked discovery. 'Didn't I go far enough? Should the neckline be lower?'

She took hold as though to pull it down but he seized her hands in his own. Instinctively her fingers tightened on his, drawing them against her skin, so that she felt him next to the swell of her breasts just before they vanished into the neckline.

He stood for a moment as though fighting to move but unable to find the strength. There was murder in his eyes.

'Damn you!' he said softly. *'Damn you, Cassie!'*

He wrenched his hands free and stormed off without waiting for her to reply. She clutched the wall, her chest rising and falling as conflicting emotions raced through her. The signals coming from him had been of violence and hostility but, far from fearing him, she was full of triumph.

He recognised her. He'd admitted it.

He'd blurted it out against his better judgement and they both knew it. Whatever the future held, thus far the battle was hers.

As she turned the corner she saw that he was still there, standing by the door through which they must go. He offered her his arm without meeting her eyes, and together they went on their way.

The others were waiting for them just inside the restaurant, agog with curiosity, but their polite smiles acted as masks and curiosity went unsatisfied. Monsieur Lenoir pulled out a chair, indicating for her to sit beside him, and Henri nimbly seized the place on her other side. For a moment she thought Marcel would say something, but Brigitte touched his cheek and he hastened to smile at her.

Cassie looked about her, fascinated. Chandeliers hung from the ceiling, golden ornaments hung from the walls. The glasses were of the finest crystal, just as the champagne being poured into them was also the finest.

She wasn't usually impressed by luxury, having seen much of it in earlier years, but there was an elegance about this place that appealed to her. She sipped the champagne appreciatively, then took a notebook from her bag and began to scribble.

'What are you doing?' Henri murmured in a tone that suggested conspiracy.

'Observing,' she said briskly. 'That's what I'm here for.'

'Surely not,' he murmured. 'You're here to have a wonderful time with a man who admires you more than any other woman in the world.'

'No, I'm here to do a job,' she said severely. 'Monsieur Falcon has employed me for my efficiency—'

'Ah, but efficiency at what?' His eyes, raking her shape left no doubt of his meaning.

'At business matters,' she informed him in her best 'prison-wardress' voice.

'But there's business and business,' he pointed out. 'It's not just facts and figures he wants from you, I'll bet.'

'Monsieur Lenoir!' she exclaimed.

'Henri, please. I already feel that we know each other well.'

'Henri, I'm shocked!'

'And I'll bet you don't shock easily. Do go on.'

'You cannot know me well if you think *that* of me.'

'Think what of you?' he asked with an innocence that would have fooled anyone not forewarned. 'I don't know what you mean.'

'I'm sure you do.'

'Well, perhaps. I can't imagine Marcel wasting you on business efficiency when you have so many other lavish talents. He's known as a man with an eye for the ladies.'

He inclined his head slightly to where Marcel was sitting. Cassie waited for him to glance across at her, disapproving

of Henri's attention, but he didn't. He seemed engrossed by
Brigitte, sitting beside him, his eyes fixed on her as though
nothing else existed in the world. Suddenly he smiled into her
eyes and Cassie had to check a gasp. Surely no man smiled
at a woman like that unless he meant it with all his heart?

There was a welcome distraction in choosing the food,
which was of the high standard she'd expected. While they ate
Henri surprised her by talking sensibly. Her questions about
Paris received knowledgeable answers and she was able to
listen with such genuine interest that when Marcel spoke to
her across the table she failed to hear him.

'I'm sorry…what…?' she stammered.

'I was merely recommending the wine,' he said. 'It's a rare
vintage and a speciality of this hotel.'

'Of course, yes. Thank you.'

'Never mind him,' Henri said. 'Let me finish telling you—'

'You've had your turn,' Monsieur Lenoir objected. 'I may
be an old man, but I'm not too old to appreciate a beautiful
woman.' He gave a rich chuckle. Liking him, Cassie gave him
her most gracious smile and they were soon deep in conversation. On the surface he was more civilised and restrained
than his son, but his observations about Paris tended to linger on the shadowy romantic places. Clearly Henri wasn't
her only admirer.

At last an orchestra struck up and dancers took to the
floor. Monsieur Lenoir extended his hand and she followed
him cheerfully.

He was a reasonably good dancer for his age and weight,
but what he really wanted, as she soon discovered, was to
flaunt his sexy young companion, enjoying envious gazes
from other men. She laughed and indulged him, careful not
to go too far, and they finally left the floor, laughing together
in perfect accord.

Henri was waiting for them, looking theatrically forlorn.

'I'm all alone,' he mourned. 'You've got my father. Marcel and Brigitte look like they're set up for the night.'

'Yes, they do, don't they,' Cassie said, observing them from a distance, dancing with eyes only for each other.

'So when will it be my turn?' Henri wanted to know.

'Right now,' she said firmly. 'Do you mind my leaving you alone?' This was to Monsieur Lenoir.

'No, you two young things go and enjoy yourself. I'm puffed.'

Before she knew it she was spinning around the floor. Henri was a good dancer. So was she, she suddenly remembered. How long had it been since she'd had the chance to let go and really enjoy herself?

For a little while she gave herself up to the thrill of moving fast. Her mind seemed to be linked to Henri, so that when he waggled his hips she instinctively did the same, and heard cheers and applause from the rest of the floor. The world was spinning by in a series of visions. They came and went in her consciousness, but the one that was always there was Marcel, watching her with narrowed, furious eyes. No matter how often she turned, he always seemed to be directly in front of her. She blinked and he vanished. And yet he was still there, because he was always there.

As the dance ended there was a mini riot, with Henri indicating that he wanted to partner her again, and at least three other men prepared to challenge for the privilege. But they all backed off when they saw Marcel, with murder in his eyes, stretching out his hand to her.

'My dance, I think,' he said.

His voice was soft but dangerous, and tonight danger had an edge that she relished.

'I don't think so,' she said with a challenging glance at her other suitors. 'I think you have to wait your turn.'

It was a crazy thing to say but she couldn't have stopped

herself for anything in the world. Suddenly she felt herself yanked fiercely against him, his arm so tight about her that she was breathless.

'I wait for no man,' he said. Then, in a voice even softer and more menacing than before, he added, 'And no woman.'

'Then I guess I have no choice,' she said. 'Let's go.'

The music had slowed, enabling him to draw her onto the floor in a waltz, his body moving against hers. She tried not to feel the rising excitement. That was to be her weapon against him, not his against her. But the shocking truth was that he was equally armed and her defences were weak. Now her only hope of standing up to him was not to let him suspect her weakness.

She reckoned a suit of armour would have been useful: something made of steel to protect her from the awareness of his body so dangerously close to hers. Lacking it, she could only assume the nearest thing to a visor, a beaming, rigid smile that should have alarmed him.

'I don't think you should hold me so tightly,' she said.

'Don't try to fool me,' he murmured in soft rage. 'This is exactly what you meant to happen.'

'You do me an injustice. I was going to wear something more conventional but you arrived before I could change.'

'Oh, please, try to think of something better.'

'Why must you always judge me so harshly?'

'If you don't know the answer to that—*mon dieu,* you're enjoying this, aren't you?'

'That's not fair.'

'When is the truth fair? I know how your deceiving little mind works—'

'How can you be so sure you know about me—a woman you met only a few days ago?'

His face was livid and she thought for a moment he would

do something violent. But he only dropped his head so that his mouth was close to her ear. *'Ne me tourmente pas ou je vais vous faire désolé. Prenez garde pendant qu'il est encore temps....'*

She drew in her breath. He'd warned her against tormenting him, telling her to take heed while there was still time.

'Don't torment me,' he groaned again. 'I warn you—I warn you—'

'Why?' she challenged. 'Whatever will happen?'

'Wait and see.'

'Suppose I can't wait. Suppose I'm impatient. What will you do then?'

'Wait and see,' he repeated with slow, deliberate emphasis.

She smiled. 'I'll look forward to that.'

His hand had been drifting lower until it almost rested on the satin curve of her behind. Suddenly he snatched it back, as though in fear, though whether of her or himself perhaps, neither of them could have said.

'Witch!' he breathed.

She chuckled. 'Anything you say. After all, you're my employer. Your word is law. I exist only to obey.'

Now his eyes were those of a man driven beyond endurance, and she really thought he would explode. But it lasted only a moment, then his steely control was in place again.

'I'm glad you realise that,' he said. 'There are things I won't tolerate.'

'You must tell me what they are,' she challenged.

His gaze was fierce and desperate. What would he say? she wondered. Was this her moment?

But the music was drawing to a close. The moment was over.

'Later,' he growled.

'Later,' she agreed.

'But soon.'

'Yes. Soon.' Her eyes met his. 'Because we've waited long enough.'

FREE Merchandise is 'in the Cards' for you!

Dear Reader,

We're giving away FREE MERCHANDISE!

Seriously, we'd like to reward you for reading this novel by giving you **FREE MERCHANDISE** worth over $20. And no purchase is necessary!

You see the Jack of Hearts sticker above? Paste that sticker in the box on the Free Merchandise Voucher inside. Return the Voucher promptly...and we'll send you valuable Free Merchandise!

Thanks again for reading one of our novels—and enjoy your Free Merchandise with our compliments!

Pam Powers

Pam Powers

H-R-02/12

P.S. Look inside to see what Free Merchandise is **"in the cards"** for you!

We'd like to send you two free books to introduce you to the Harlequin® Romance series. These books are worth over $10, but they are yours to keep absolutely FREE! We'll even send you 2 wonderful surprise gifts. You can't lose!

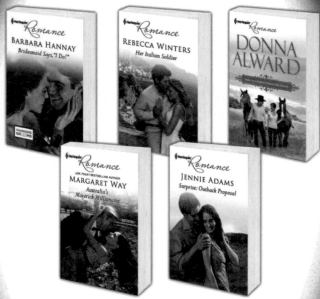

REMEMBER: Your Free Merchandise, consisting of **2 Free Books** and **2 Free Gifts**, is worth over $20.00! No purchase is necessary, so please send for your Free Merchandise today.

Plus TWO FREE GIFTS!

We'll also send you two wonderful FREE GIFTS (worth about $10), in addition to your 2 Free Harlequin® Romance books!

Visit us at:

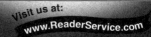

www.ReaderService.com

YOUR FREE MERCHANDISE INCLUDES...

2 FREE Harlequin® Romance Books

AND 2 FREE Mystery Gifts

FREE MERCHANDISE VOUCHER

2 FREE
BOOKS
and
2 FREE
GIFTS

Please send my Free Merchandise, consisting of
2 Free Books and **2 Free Mystery Gifts.**
I understand that I am under no obligation to buy
anything, as explained on the back of this card.

❏ I prefer the regular-print edition
116/316 HDL FMN5

❏ I prefer the larger-print edition
186/386 HDL FMN5

Please Print

FIRST NAME

LAST NAME

ADDRESS

APT.#   CITY

STATE/PROV.   ZIP/POSTAL CODE

NO PURCHASE NECESSARY!

De ach card and mail today. No stamp needed. ▶

▶ © 2011 HARLEQUIN ENTERPRISES LIMITED ® and ™ are trademarks owned and used by the trademark owner and/or its licensee. Printed in the U.S.A.

HR0412

The Reader Service - Here's how it works:

BUSINESS REPLY MAIL

FIRST-CLASS MAIL   PERMIT NO. 717   BUFFALO, NY

POSTAGE WILL BE PAID BY ADDRESSEE

THE READER SERVICE

PO BOX 1867

BUFFALO NY 14240-9952

NO POSTAGE
NECESSARY
IF MAILED
IN THE
UNITED STATES

CHAPTER SEVEN

POLITELY they walked each other off the floor, slowing suddenly as they came within sight of the table.

'Oh, no!' Marcel groaned.

Cassie didn't need to ask about the newcomer. A woman in her thirties, tense, angular and furious, sat next to Henri, hectoring him as only a wife would have done.

'You found another floozie fast enough. I've been watching you dance with her.' Her eyes fell on the blonde bombshell approaching the table on Marcel's arm, and an expression of contempt overtook her face. 'And here she is.' She rose and confronted Cassie.

'Got another one, have you? Finished with my Henri, think this one'll have more money? That's how your kind operate, isn't it? Find out what they're worth and move from one to the other.' She glared at Marcel. 'Don't fool yourself. When she meets a man with more cash you'll be history. Don't suppose you know what it's like to be dumped, do you? Well, you'll find out with her.'

The air was singing about Cassie's head. How would Marcel respond to these words that seemed to home in on his own experience with such deadly accuracy?

His reply amazed her.

'Good evening, Madame Lenoir. I am so glad you could join your husband.'

'Join him? I'm going to get rid of him for good. I saw him dancing with *her,* and what an exhibition that was! Now she can have him.'

'You are mistaken, *madame,*' Marcel said coolly. 'Mrs Henshaw danced with your husband only out of courtesy. She is with me tonight, and I would prefer it if you did not insult her.'

'Oh, would you? Well, I'd prefer it if—'

She got no further. Scenting danger, Henri started to draw her away, apologizing frantically. When they had gone there were sighs of relief. Monsieur Lenoir indicated for Cassie to sit beside him but she'd had as much as she could stand.

'Forgive me,' she said, 'but I'm rather tired. I just want to go to bed. I'll be at work first thing tomorrow morning. Goodnight.'

She was backing away hastily as she spoke, giving Marcel no chance to object. Not that he wanted to, she thought. He must be glad to be rid of her.

In her room she stripped off, showered and dressed for the night. Her pyjamas were 'Mrs Henshaw', plain linen, loose trousers, high buttons.

Stick to Mrs Henshaw in future, she thought. You could argue that Cassie hadn't been a success.

Or you could argue that she'd been so much of a success that it had put the cat among the pigeons.

She paced the floor, too agitated to sleep. Everything that had happened this evening had been unexpected. She'd coped with surprise after surprise, and the biggest surprise of all had been Marcel's defence of her.

But it hadn't been personal, she thought with a sigh. Only what conventional courtesy demanded. If only…

There came a sharp knock on her door.

'Who is it?' she called.

'Me.' It was Marcel. He tried the door, rattling it. 'Open the door.'

She did so. Instantly his hand appeared, preventing her closing it if she'd wanted to. But she didn't want to. This moment had been too long in coming, and now she was ready for it with all guns blazing.

He pushed in so fast that she had to back away. His eyes darted around the room.

'I'm alone,' she said ironically. 'Henri left tamely with his wife. He didn't come flying back to me, whatever you think.'

'You'll pardon me if I don't take your word for that.'

'No, I won't pardon you,' she said. 'I'm not a liar. There's nobody here but us.'

He ignored her. He was opening doors, looking into the bathroom, the wardrobe. Her temper rose sharply.

'Look at me,' she said, indicating her dull attire. 'Do you think any woman entertains a lover dressed in clothes like this?'

'That depends how long she means to wear them. When she knows he'll rip them off her as soon as possible—'

'Is that what Henri wanted?' she asked sarcastically. 'He didn't say.'

'He didn't need to. It's what he wanted and every man in the room wanted. That's the truth and we both know it.'

'Now, look—'

He turned on her in swift fury. 'Don't take me for a fool!'

'But you are a fool,' she raged. 'The biggest fool in creation. Hey, what do you think you're doing?'

'Locking the door so that we're not disturbed. Since the conversation is getting down to basics, I have things to say to you.'

'I think we both have things to say.'

He nodded. 'Yes, and they've waited too long, *Mrs Henshaw*.'

For a moment she didn't speak. Then she said quietly, 'Are you sure that's what you want to call me?'

'I don't want to call you anything. I'd rather not have to endure the sight of you. I thought you were safely out of my life, just a bitter, evil memory that I could kick aside. But now—' He checked himself and looked her up and down, breathing hard with the emotion that threatened to overwhelm him.

'It is you, isn't it?' he said at last.

It was the question he'd promised himself not to ask, because that would be a sign of yielding. But now he knew there had never been a choice.

'It is you,' he repeated.

'You've known that all along.'

'I thought so—sometimes I wasn't sure—it didn't seem possible that you could be—' He broke off, breathing harshly. 'I've tried not to believe it,' he said at last.

'So you didn't want it to be true?'

'Of course I didn't,' he said with soft violence. 'Why should I want to meet you again? I can still hardly comprehend— what evil design made you come after me?'

'Don't flatter yourself,' she cried angrily. 'I didn't seek you out. I went to see Marcel Falcon. Until I saw you I had no idea it was the man I'd known as Marcel Degrande. If I *had* known I'd never have gone to that meeting. When I recognised you I ran away as fast as I could.'

'But you turned back.'

'I didn't mean to. At first I ran into the garden, but to finally escape I had to come back through the hotel and I met you coming out. Don't you understand? *I* didn't want to see *you* again. There was just too much—'

Suddenly the words choked her, and she turned away with a helpless gesture.

'Yes,' he growled. 'Too much. We could never have met peacefully.' He took hold of her and twisted her around.

'Don't turn your back on me. You flaunted your charms tonight, and I endured it, but no more! Did it please you to taunt and jeer at me?'

'I wasn't—' She tried to free herself but he gripped her more tightly.

'Don't lie. You knew exactly what you were doing to me, wearing those—those—you know what I mean. What kind of twisted pleasure did it give you? Or don't I need to ask? You played your games, the way you've always done—'

'I never played games with you,' she said desperately.

'Oh, but you did. You just weren't so frank about it in those days. Sweet, loving little Cassie, wide-eyed and innocent, honestly in love. And I believed it. Until I discovered that you were heartless, incapable of honest love. That was a useful lesson. Once learned, never forgotten. That's the Cassie I knew. So tell me, who is Mrs Henshaw?'

'She's who I am now,' she cried. 'At least I thought so. I thought Cassie had died a long time ago.'

'But tonight she rose again, didn't she? Because some creatures never die. You showed me that nothing had changed, and stood back laughing at the result. I hope I didn't disappoint you.'

'Can that be true?' she challenged him. 'That nothing has changed?'

She heard his swift intake of breath, saw the wild look in his eyes and knew that she'd hit a nerve. He didn't reply. He couldn't. So she answered for him.

'Of course it isn't true, Marcel. It *can't* be true.'

'You said yourself that Cassie hadn't really died,' he reminded her coldly.

'But she's not the same Cassie. She's seen things she never thought to see, things she didn't want to see, but can't forget. She's trapped in her own memories. What about you?'

His terrible expression was her answer. It was the look of a man struggling to get free, knowing he was doomed to fail.

'I can cope with memories,' he said. 'But from some things there's no escape.'

'If you're accusing me of pursuing you, I've already explained—'

'I'm not. Not the way you mean.'

She had pursued him in dreams and fantasies, visions and nightmares. He'd tried to drive her off, crying out that he hated and despised her—that if they met again he would take revenge. But her ghost laughed at his rage, jeered that she was stronger than he, and haunted him so relentlessly that when she'd actually risen before his eyes it was as though he'd summoned her by the force of his will.

He knew he shouldn't tell her this. It would give her too much power, and her power was already alarming. But he couldn't stop himself saying, 'You were always there. A million times I tried to make you go, but you wouldn't. Now you're really here, and I'm no longer a callow boy to let you trick me and run.'

'Why must you think the worst of me?' she cried.

'Haven't I reason? Didn't you desert me when I was almost at death's door?'

'No, I didn't desert you,' she cried. 'I did it for you—'

'Surely you can think of something better than that,' he sneered.

'It's true. I had no choice.'

'You're lying and it's not even a clever lie. Anyone could see through it.'

'Listen to me—' she screamed.

'No, you listen to me. I hate you, Cassie, or Mrs Henshaw, whoever you are today. I shall hate you as long as I live. There's only one thing about you that I don't hate, and it's this.'

He pulled her hard against him and looked down into her face. She felt his hands move away from her shoulders to take her head, holding it in the right position so that she couldn't resist. She knew what he was about to do, but nothing could prepare her for the feel of his lips on hers after so long.

'Marcel,' she gasped.

'You've been trying to drive me insane all evening, and now you've done it. Are you pleased? Is this what you wanted?'

It was exactly what she wanted and only now did she admit the truth to herself. All her anger and defiance had been heading for this moment, trying to drive him to take her into his arms. Her body, her senses and, if she were honest, her heart, had been set on this, and if he'd resisted her it would have been an insult for which she would never have forgiven him. A sigh broke from her, and her warm breath against his mouth inflamed him more. He deepened the kiss with his tongue, seeking her response, sensing it, driven wild by it.

Her arms seemed to move of their own accord, gliding up around his neck, holding, drawing his head fiercely against hers, sending him a message with her lips and tongue.

But suddenly he drew back as though forcing himself with a great effort.

'Tell me to stop,' he growled. 'Tell me. Let me hear you say it.'

'How can I?' she said huskily. 'You never took orders from me.'

'You never needed to give me orders. I did what you wanted without you having to say it.'

'You were always so sure you knew what I wanted,' she murmured, looking up with teasing eyes that were as provocative as she meant them to be.

'You never complained.'

'Perhaps I was afraid of you.'

'*You?*' he echoed in a voice that was almost savage. 'Afraid of *me?*'

'Perhaps I'm afraid of you now. I'm in your power, aren't I?'

'Then tell me to stop,' he repeated with grim emphasis.

For answer she gave him a smile that tested his self control to the limit. She felt the tremor go through him, and smiled again.

'Tell me to stop!' he said desperately.

'Do *you* think you should stop?' she whispered.

'Damn you! *Damn you!*'

His hands were moving feverishly, finding the buttons of her pyjamas, wrenching them open, tossing the puritanical jacket aside. He touched her breasts with his fingers, then his lips, groaning softly so that his warm breath whispered over her skin, sending a frisson of delight through her.

She was aware of him moving towards the bedroom, taking her with him, but then all sensations merged until she felt the bed beneath her. He raised his head to gaze down at her and she instinctively began to work on his buttons, ripping them open even faster than he had ripped hers.

It was dark in this room and all they could see of each other was their eyes, fierce and gleaming with mutual desire. And then the moment came. After so many years they were one again, moving in a perfect physical harmony that defied their antagonism. The old memories were still alive, how to please each other, inflame each other, challenge, defy, infuriate each other. And then how to lie quietly in each other's arms, feeling the roar die away, leaving only fulfilment behind.

She could barely make out his features, but she sensed his confusion. For once in his life, Marcel was lost for words. She gave him a reassuring smile.

'Would you really have stopped if I'd asked you?' she murmured.

A long silence.

'Let's just say…I'm glad you didn't ask me,' he said at last, slowly.

She waited for him to say more. Whatever the past, they had suddenly discovered a new road that could lead back to each other. Surely now he would have words of tenderness for her?

Full of hope, she reached out, brushing her fingertips against his face.

But he drew back sharply, stared at her for a moment, then rose from the bed like a man fleeing the devil.

'No,' he said softly, then violently, *'no!'*

'Marcel—'

'No!' he repeated, then gave a sudden bitter laugh. 'Oh, *mon dieu!'* He laughed again, but there was no humour in it, only a grating edge.

'Look at me. How easily I…well done, Cassie. You won the first battle. I'll win the others but it's the first one that counts, isn't it? Did you hear me on the dance floor tonight, saying I waited for no woman? That has to be the biggest and stupidest piece of self deception of all time. All those years ago I waited for you—waited and waited, certain that you would come in the end because my Cassie loved me. Waited… waited…' He broke off with a shudder.

So the past couldn't be dealt with so easily, she thought. She must tell him everything, help him to understand that she'd had no choice but to save him from harm. But surely it would be easier now?

'Marcel, listen to me. I must tell you—'

But he couldn't hear her. He'd leapt up and was pacing about, talking frantically, lost in another world. Or perhaps trapped in a cage.

'Once I wouldn't have believed it possible to despise any-one as I've despised you. In those days I loved you more than my life, more than—' He stopped and a violent tremor went through him. 'Never mind that,' he said harshly.

'I guess you don't want to remember that we loved each other.'

'I said never mind,' he shouted. 'And don't talk about "each other". There was no love on your side, or you could never have done what you did.'

'You don't know what I did,' she cried.

'I know that I lay for days in the hospital, longing to see you. I was delirious, dreaming of you, certain that the next time I opened my eyes you'd be there. But you never were.

'I called your mobile phone but it was always switched off. The phone in your apartment was never answered. Tell me, Cassie, didn't you ever wonder why I vanished so suddenly? You never wanted to ask a single question?'

She stared. 'But I knew what had happened, that you'd had an accident and were in hospital. I told you that in my letter.'

'What letter?'

'I wrote, telling you everything, begging you to under-stand that it wasn't my fault. I put it through your door—I was sure you'd find it when you came home. Oh heavens! Do you mean—?'

'I never read any letter from you,' he said, and she was too distracted to notice how carefully he chose his words.

'Then you never knew that I was forced to leave you—I had no choice.'

He made a sound of impatience. 'Don't tell me things that a child couldn't believe. Of course there was a choice.'

'Not if I wanted you to live,' she cried. 'He said he'd kill you.'

'He? Who?'

'Jake Simpson.'

'Who the hell—?'

'I'd never heard of him either. He was a crook who knew how to keep his head down. People did what he wanted because they were scared of him. I wasn't scared at first. When he said he wanted me I told him to clear off. You were away at the time. I was going to tell you when you got home, but you had the accident. Only it wasn't an accident. Jake arranged it to warn me. He showed me a picture of you in hospital and said you'd die if I didn't drop you and turn to him. I couldn't even tell you what had happened because if I tried to visit you he'd know, and you'd have another "accident".

'I went with him because I had to. I didn't dare approach you, but I couldn't endure thinking of you believing that I'd played you false. In the end I wrote a letter and slipped it through your letter box. Obviously you never got it. Perhaps you'd already left by then. Oh, if only you could have read it. We'd still have been apart, but you'd have known that I didn't betray you, that I was forced to do what I did, and perhaps you wouldn't have hated me.'

She looked at him, standing quite still in the shadows.

'Or maybe you'd have hated me anyway. All these years—'

'Stop,' he said harshly. 'Don't say any more.'

'No, well, I guess there's no more to say. If I could turn back the clock I'd put that letter into your hands and make you read it and then perhaps I wouldn't have been such a monster in your heart—'

'I said stop!' he shouted.

She came to a sudden resolution. Reaching up from where she was sitting on the bed, she took his hand and urged him down until he was sitting beside her.

'You don't know whether to believe me or not, do you? Everything about us is different—except for one thing. Very well. If that's the only way I can make you listen to me, then that's the way I'll take.'

'Meaning?'

'You've implied that I'm a bad woman who'll use her physical charms to get her way with you. Well, maybe you're right. After all, I know now that I can do it, don't I?'

'What are you saying?'

'That I'll do what I have to. Maybe you know me better than I know myself. Perhaps I really am that unscrupulous. Maybe I'll enjoy it. Maybe we both will.'

As she spoke she was touching his face. She knew she was taking a huge risk, but there was no other way. At all costs she would soften him, drive the hostility from his eyes.

To her relief she could feel him softening, feel the hostile tension drain from him, replaced by a different kind of tension.

'Hold me,' she whispered.

He did so, reaching for her, drawing her down to stretch out on the bed, or letting her draw him down. Neither of them really knew.

Their first encounter had been entirely sexual. This one was on a different plane. No words were spoken, but none were needed. In each other's arms they seemed to find again the things that had been missing the first time—sweetness, warmth, the joy of the heart.

Afterwards they held each other with gentle hands.

'We'll get there,' she promised. 'We'll find a way, my darling, I promise we will.'

He didn't reply, and she suddenly became aware that his breathing was deep and steady. She turned her head, the better to see his face, and gave a tender smile as she saw him sunk in sleep.

It had always been this way, she remembered. He would love her with all the power and vigour of a great man, then fall asleep like a child.

'That's right, you sleep,' she murmured. 'Sleep and I'll take care of everything.'

Slowly her smile changed. Now it was one of triumph.

In the twilight world that came just before awakening she relived a dream. So many times she'd fallen asleep in his arms, knowing that he would still be there in the morning. Sometimes she'd opened her eyes to find him looking down at her adoringly. At other times he would be sunk in sleep, but always reaching for her, even if only with his fingertips. It was as though he could only relax with the assurance of her presence.

And me, she thought hazily, *knowing he would be there meant that life was good.*

She opened her eyes.

She was alone.

He was gone.

She sat up, looking around frantically, certain that there was some mistake. The room was empty. Hurrying out of bed, she searched all the rooms but there was no sign of him. Marcel had stolen away while she slept.

But he'd vowed to keep her a prisoner. The outer door would be locked.

It wasn't. It yielded at once and she found herself looking out into an empty corridor. Something about the silence was frightening.

She slammed the door and leaned back against it, refusing to believe that this could have happened. Last night they'd found each other again, not totally but enough for hope. They should have spent today talking, repairing the past. Instead he'd walked out.

But he might have fled through caution, she thought. Don't judge him until you've spoken to him.

She dressed carefully. Cassie or Mrs Henshaw today?

Finally she settled on a mixture, restrained clothing as befitted her job, but with her hair flowing freely. He would understand. A quick breakfast and she was ready to face whatever the challenge was.

The door to Marcel's apartment was opened by a middle-aged woman with a friendly face.

'*Bonjour.* I am Vera, Marcel's secretary. He has left me instructions to be of service to you.'

'Left you—? Isn't he here?'

'He had to leave suddenly. For what reason he did not say. I'm a little surprised because he has so much to do, and he didn't even tell me where he was going.'

So that was that. He was snubbing her, escaping to some place where she couldn't follow. Perhaps she should simply take the hint and leave, but that seemed too much like giving in without a fight. How he would triumph if he returned to find her gone. Grimly she settled down to work.

CHAPTER EIGHT

LAURA Degrande had settled contentedly in a small house in the suburbs of Paris. It wasn't a wealthy district, but she always said life was better without wealth. Her marriage to Amos Falcon had not been happy, and the only good thing to come from it was her son, Marcel. He would have kept her in luxury, but she refused, accepting an allowance that was comfortable, but no more, despite his indignant protests. It was the only blot on their otherwise affectionate relationship.

Her face lit up when he appeared at her door.

'My darling, how lovely to see you. I was thrilled to get your call this morning. What is it that's so urgent?'

Hugging her, Marcel said, 'I need to look through some old stuff that you stored for me.'

'Have you lost something?'

'You might say that. Are the bags where I left them?'

'Still in the attic.'

'See you later.'

He hurried up the stairs before she could answer, and shut himself away in the little room, where he began to pull open bags and boxes, tossing them aside when they didn't contain what he wanted. When Laura looked in he turned a haggard face towards her.

'There's something missing—a big grey envelope—I left it here—it's gone—'

'Oh, that. Yes, I found it but there was only rubbish inside, shreds of paper that you'd obviously torn up. I thought they should be thrown out.'

'What?' The sound that broke from him was a roar of anguish. His face was haggard, desperate. 'You threw it out?'

'No, calm down. I thought about it but then I remembered what you're like about not throwing things away. So I stored them safely—up here on this shelf. Yes, here's the envelope.'

He almost snatched it from her with a choking, 'Thank you!'

Laura left the room quickly, knowing that something desperately important had happened, and he needed to be alone to cope with it.

Marcel wrenched open the envelope and a load of small bits of paper cascaded onto the floor. Frantically he gathered them up, found a small table and began to piece them together. It was hard because his hands were shaking, and the paper had been torn into tiny shreds.

As he worked he could see himself again, on that night long ago, tearing, tearing, desperate with hate and misery.

He'd left the hospital as soon as he was strong enough, and gone straight to Cassie's home. The lights were out and he knew the worst as soon as he arrived, but he still banged on the door, crying her name, banging more desperately.

'You're wasting your time,' said a voice behind him. 'She's gone.'

Behind him stood a middle-aged man who Marcel knew vaguely. He was usually grumpy, but today he seemed pleased at the bad news he was imparting.

'Gone where?' Marcel demanded.

A shrug. 'How do I know? She packed up and left days ago. I saw her get into a posh car. Bloke who owned it must be a millionaire, so I reckon that's finished you. She saw sense at last.'

Seeing Marcel's face, he retreated hastily.

At first he refused to believe it, banging on the door again and screaming her name, until at last even he had to accept the truth. She'd gone without a backward glance.

He didn't remember the journey home, except that he sat drinking in the back of the taxi until he tumbled out onto the pavement and staggered into the building.

On the mat he found an envelope, with his name in Cassie's handwriting. The sight had been enough to make him explode with drunken rage and misery, tearing it, tearing, tearing, tearing—until only shreds were left.

He'd left England next morning. At the airport he'd had a brief glimpse of Cassie, dressed up to the nines, in the company of a man who clearly had money coming out of his ears. That sight answered all his questions. He'd screamed abuse, and fled.

In Paris he'd taken refuge in his mother's home, collapsing and letting her care for him. When he unpacked it was actually a surprise to discover that he'd brought Cassie's letter, although in shreds. He had no memory of putting it into his bag.

Now was the time to destroy it finally, but he hesitated. Better to keep it, and read it one day, years ahead. When he was an old man, ruling a financial empire, with an expensive wife and a gang of children, then he would read the whore's miserable excuses.

And laugh.

How he would laugh! He'd laugh as violently as he was weeping now.

When at last he could control his sobs he took the bits of paper to his room, stuffed them into an envelope and put it in a drawer by his bed. There it had stayed until he'd moved out. Then he'd hidden it away in the little attic, asking his mother to be sure never to touch his things.

As the years passed he'd sometimes thought of the day that would come when he could read her pathetic words and jeer at her memory. Now that day was here.

He worked feverishly, fixing the pieces together. But gradually his tension increased. Something was wrong. No, it was impossible. Be patient! It would come right.

But at last he could no longer delude himself. With every tiny wisp of paper scrutinised to no avail, with every last chance gone, he slammed his fist into the wall again and again.

When there was no word, and her calls went unanswered, Cassie came to a final reluctant decision. As she packed she chided herself for imagining that things could ever have been different. Her flesh was still warm from their encounters the night before, but she should never have fooled herself.

He was punishing her by abandoning her in the way he felt she'd abandoned him. The generous person he'd once been would never have taken such cruel, carefully thought out vengeance, but now he was a different man, one she didn't know.

She called the airport and booked herself onto the evening flight to London. There! It was done.

'You are leaving?' asked Vera, who'd been listening.

'Yes, I have to. Would you please give this to Marcel?' She handed over a sealed envelope. Inside was a small piece of paper, on which she'd written: *'It's better this way. I'm sure you agree. Cassie.'*

'Can't you wait just a little?' Vera begged.

'No, I've stayed too long already.'

Take-off was not for three hours but she felt an urgent need to get away at once. She took a taxi to the airport and sat, trying not to brood. She should never have come to this place, never dreamed that the terrible wrongs of the past could be put right. How triumphant he would feel, knowing his snub had driven her away! How glad he would be to be rid of her!

At last it was time to check in. She rose and joined the queue. She had almost reached the front when a yell rent the air.

'Cassie!'

Everyone looked up to see the man standing at the top of a flight of stairs, but he saw none of them. His eyes were fixed only on her as he hurled himself down at breakneck speed and ran to her so fast that he had to seize her in order to steady himself.

'What do you think you're doing?' he demanded frantically.

'I'm going home.'

'You're staying here.'

'Let go of me.'

'No!' He was holding her in an unbreakable grip 'You can either agree to come back with me, or we can fight it out right here and now. Which?'

'You're impossible!'

'It took you ten years to discover that? I thought you were clever. Yes or no?'

'All right—yes.'

'Good. Is this yours?' He lifted her suitcase with one hand while still holding her wrist with the other. Plainly he was taking no chances.

In this awkward fashion they made it out of the building to where the car from La Couronne was waiting for them. While the chauffeur loaded the suitcase Marcel guided her into the back and drew the glass partition across, isolating them. As the car sped through the Paris traffic he kept hold of her hand.

'There's no need to grip me so tightly,' she said. 'I'm hardly going to jump out here.'

'I'm taking no chances. You could vanish at any time. You've done it twice, you won't do it to me again. You can count on that.'

'I went because you made it so obvious that you wanted to be rid of me.'

'Are you mad?' he demanded.

'I'm not the one who vanished into thin air. When a woman awakes to find the man gone in the morning that's a pretty clear message.'

'Tell me about vanishing into thin air,' he growled. 'You're the expert.'

'I left a note with Vera—'

I didn't mean today.' The words came out as a cry of pain, and she cursed herself for stupidity.

'No, I guess not. I'm sorry. So when you left this morning, that was your way of paying me back?'

'I went because I had to, but…things happened. I never meant to stay away so long. When I got back and Vera told me you'd left for England I couldn't believe it. I tried to call you but you'd turned your phone off—*like last time.'*

She drew a sharp breath. Something in his voice, his eyes, revealed all his suffering as no mere words could have done.

'But why did you have to dash off?' she asked.

'To read the letter you wrote me ten years ago.'

'But you said you never got it.'

'No, I said I never read it. I was so blazing mad I tore it up without reading it.'

'Then how could you read it now?'

'Because I kept it,' he said savagely. 'Fool that I am, I kept it.'

She could hardly believe her ears. 'And you never—in all these years—?'

'No, I never read it. But neither did I throw it away. Today I went to my mother's home where it's been stored, meaning to fit it together. But it isn't all there. Some of the pieces are lost. I came straight back to find you, and you were gone. Vera heard you booking the flight so I had to act fast.'

'You only just got there in time,' she murmured.

'Well, actually—I have a friend who works in airport security. I called him. You wouldn't have been allowed to get on that plane.'

'*What?* You actually dared—?'

'I couldn't risk you getting away. It's too important.'

'And suppose I want to get away?'

He looked at her in silence. Words could never have said so clearly that what she wanted played no part in this. This was a man driven by demons that were too strong for him, and perhaps also for her.

'So you want me to explain the missing pieces?' she guessed.

'If you can remember them.'

'Oh, yes,' she murmured. 'I can remember everything.'

They had reached La Couronne. Marcel hurried her inside, his hand still on her arm. Several people tried to attract his attention, but he never saw them. Only one thing mattered now.

As soon as they were inside his apartment he locked the door. She almost told him there was no need, but then kept silent. Marcel was in the grip of an obsession and she, of all people, couldn't say it was irrational. She knew a burst of pity for him, standing on the edge of a dangerous pit. If he fell into its fearsome depths, wouldn't she be at least partly to blame?

He held out the letter, where she could see tiny scraps stuck onto a base sheet, but with gaping holes.

'Do you recognise this?' he demanded.

'Yes, of course.'

He thrust it into her hands and turned away. 'Read it to me.'

It felt weird to see the words over which she'd struggled so hard and wept so many tears. She began to read aloud.

"'My darling, beloved Marcel, you will wonder why I didn't come to you when you were in pain and trouble, but I didn't dare. What happened wasn't an accident. It was done on purpose by a man who wants to claim me for himself. I refused him, and—'" She stopped. 'There's a gap here.'

'What are the missing words?' he asked.

She closed her eyes, travelling back to the past. *"'He hurt you, to show me what would happen if I didn't give in,'"* she said slowly. She opened her eyes.

'Then the letter goes on, *"I couldn't risk coming to you in the hospital because he would have known and he might kill you. I'm delivering this through your door, because it's the only way I can think of that he won't find out. I hope and pray that it will be safe. I couldn't bear it if you believed I'd just walked away, or stopped loving you."* Then there's another gap.'

'Do you know what's missing?' When she didn't answer he turned and repeated harshly, 'Do you?'

'Yes. I said—'*"I will never stop loving you, until the very end of my days, but this is the last time I can ever say so."'* The signature is still there if you want to read it.

'I don't need to read it,' he said quietly, and recited, *'Your very own Cassie, yours forever, however long "forever" may last.'* I don't suppose you remember writing that.'

'Yes, I remember writing every word, even the ones that aren't here any more.'

"'I will never stop loving you until the very end of my days,"' he repeated. 'You're sure you wrote that?'

'Yes, I'm quite sure. But even if you doubt me, the rest of the letter is there. I told you what had happened and why I had to leave you. If only you'd read it then, you'd have known that I still loved you—oh, Marcel—all these years!'

'Don't,' he begged, shuddering. 'If I think of that I'll go mad.'

'I'm surprised we haven't both gone mad long before this. And it was all so unnecessary.'

'Yes, if I'd read this then—'

'No, I mean more than that. There's another reason the last ten years could have been avoided.' She broke off, heaving.

'What do you mean?' he demanded.

She raised fierce eyes to his face.

'I mean that you played your part in what happened to us. It could all have been so different if only you'd been honest with me. Why didn't you tell me who you were, who your father was? We need never have been driven apart.'

He stared. 'What difference—?'

Her temper was rising fast. 'If I'd known you were the son of Amos Falcon I'd have gone to him for help. He's a powerful man. When he heard what Jake had done he would have dealt with him, had him arrested, sent to jail. We'd have been safe.

'Everything since then could have been different. You'd have been spared all that suffering and disillusion. I'd have been spared that terrible time with Jake. So much misery because you had to play a silly game.'

He tore his hair. 'I was just…I didn't want you to know I came from a rich family.'

'Because you thought I'd be too interested in your money. Charming!'

'No, because you thought I was poor and you chose me over your rich admirers. That meant the world to me—'

'Yes, but there was a high price, and you weren't the only one who paid it. You spoke of hating me, but I could hate *you* for what you did to my life with your juvenile games. When I found out the truth recently I…I just couldn't…so much misery, and so needless—*aaaargh!*'

The last word was a scream that seemed to tear itself from her body without her meaning it. It was followed by another, and another, and now she couldn't stop screaming.

'Cassie!' he tried, reaching for her. *'Cassie!'*

'Get away from me,' she screamed. 'Don't touch me. *I hate you.*'

He wouldn't let her fight him off, drawing her closer until her face was against his shoulder, murmuring in her ear, 'That's right, hate me. I deserve it. Hate me, hate me.'

'Yes,' she wept.

'I'm a damned fool and you suffered for it. Call me every name you can think of. Hit me if you like.' He drew back so that she could see his face. 'It's no more than I deserve. Go on, I won't stop you.'

She couldn't speak, just shook her head while the tears ran down her cheeks. Then she was back in his arms, held against him, feeling him pick her up, kick open a door and lay her down on a soft bed.

But this was no love-making. Lying beside her, he held her gently, murmuring soothing words, stroking her hair. Her efforts to stop weeping were in vain, and he seemed to understand this because he murmured, 'Go on, cry it out. Don't try to hold back.'

'All those wasted years,' she choked.

'Years when we could have been together,' he agreed, 'loving each other, making each other happy, having children. All gone because I was a conceited oaf.'

'No, you weren't,' she managed to say. 'You were just young—'

'Young and stupid,' he supplied. 'Not thinking of anyone but myself, imagining I could play games without people being hurt—'

'Don't be so hard on yourself,' she said huskily.

'Why not? It's true. I did it. My silly pretence meant you

couldn't seek my father's help and, even after that, if I'd only read your letter I—*imbécile, stupide!*'

'Marcel,' she wept, 'Marcel—'

Distress choked her again, but now it was the same with him. She could feel his body heaving, his arms around her as hers were around him.

'I did it,' he sobbed. 'I did it. It's all my fault.'

'No...no...' She tightened her embrace, tenderly stroking his head as a mother might have done with a child.

'Ten years,' he gasped. 'Ten years! Where did they go? How can we get them back?'

'We can't,' she said. 'What's done can never be undone.'

'I don't believe that!'

'Marcel, you can't turn the clock back; it isn't possible. We can only go on from here.'

He didn't reply in words, but she felt his arms tighten, as though he feared that she might slip away again.

Go on where? said the voice in her head. *And what do you mean by 'we'? Who are you? Who is he now?*

She silenced the voice. She had no answer to those troublesome questions. Everything she'd suffered, the lessons learned in the last ten years, all the confusion and despair, were uniting to cry with a thousand voices that from this moment nothing would be simple, nothing easy, and it might all end in more heartbreak.

It was a relief to realise that he was relaxing into sleep in her arms, as though in her he found the only true comfort. She stroked him some more, murmuring soft words in his ear. 'Sleep, my darling. We'll find a way. I only wish I knew...I wish I knew...'

But then sleep came to her rescue too, and the words faded into nothing.

It was dark when she awoke and the illuminated clock by the bed told her they had dozed for barely an hour. Careful not to awaken Marcel, she eased away and sat on the side of the bed, dropping her head into her hands, feeling drained.

The concerns that had worried her before were even stronger now. Their tumultuous discoveries could bring great happiness, or great despair. They had found each other again, and perhaps the troubles of the past could be made right. But it was too soon to be sure, and she had a strange sensation of watching everything from a distance.

She walked over to the window, looking out on the dazzling view. Paris was a blaze of light against the darkness.

'Are you all right?' came his voice from behind her.

'Yes, I'm fine,' she said quickly.

He came up behind her and she felt his hands on her shoulders. 'Are you sure? You seem very troubled.'

How had he divined that merely from her back view? she wondered. How and where had he gained such insight?

'What are you thinking?' he asked softly.

'I don't know. My thoughts come and go so quickly I can't keep up with them.'

'Me too,' he agreed. 'We must have many long talks.'

'But not now,' she said. 'I feel as though I'm choking. I need to go out into the fresh air.'

'Fine, let's go for a walk.'

'No, I have to be alone.'

'Cassie—'

'It's all right, I won't vanish again. I'll return, I promise.'

'It's dark,' he persisted. 'Do you know how late it is?'

'I have to do this,' she said in a tense voice. 'Please, Marcel, don't try to stop me.'

He was silent and she sensed his struggle. But at last he sighed and stood back to let her pass.

Without even going to her own apartment, she hurried directly down to the entrance. The hotel was close to the River Seine, and by following the signs she was able to find the way to the water. Here she could stand looking down at the little ripples, glittering through the darkness, and listen to the sounds of the city. Late as it was, Paris was still alive. Far in the distance she could see the Eiffel Tower reaching up into the heavens.

She turned around slowly and that was when she saw the man, fifty yards away along the embankment, standing quite still, watching her. At first she thought he was a stalker, but then she recognised him. Marcel.

When she began to walk towards him he backed away. When she turned and moved off he followed.

'Marcel,' she called. 'What do you think you're doing?'

At last he drew close enough for her to see a slightly sheepish look on his face.

'I was just concerned for your safety,' he responded. 'I'll keep my distance, and leave you in peace. But I'll always be there if you need me.'

Her annoyance died and she managed a shaky laugh. 'My guardian angel, huh?'

'That has to be the first time anyone's mistaken me for an angel,' he said wryly.

'Why do I find that so easy to believe? All right, you can stay.'

Recently she had forgotten how much charm he had when he was set on getting his own way. Suddenly she was remembering.

He completed the effect by taking two small wine bottles from his pockets and handing her one. 'Let's sit down,' he said.

She did so and drank the wine thankfully.

'It's a lot to take in all at once, isn't it?' he said.

'Yes, I guess so.'

'These last few years must have been terrible for you. The

man who had me run down—was that the man I saw you with at the airport?'

'Yes, that was Jake. I'd spent the previous few days at his house, "entertaining him" as he put it.'

'You don't need to say any more,' Marcel said in a strained voice.

'No, I guess not.

'We were travelling to America that day. After he'd seen you he kept on and on at me, demanding to know if I'd been in touch with you. I swore I hadn't, and in the end he believed me because he said if you'd known the truth you wouldn't have called me "Whore".

'I didn't know what to believe. I thought perhaps you'd read my letter and were pretending, or maybe you hadn't been home yet and would get it later. But I told Jake that he must be right about that.' She gave a wry smile. 'It was always wise to tell Jake he was right. He'd already destroyed my cellphone so that nobody could get in touch with me.'

'So you were his prisoner?' he said, aghast. 'All that time you were suffering and I did nothing to help you.'

'How could you? I must admit that I did hope for a while, but in the end I realised you'd accepted our parting and that was the end. So I married him.'

'You married him?'

'Why not? I felt my life was over. I just went with the tide. When I found he'd been fooling around with other women it gave me the weapon I needed to divorce him. Suddenly I wasn't afraid of him any more. I accepted some money from him because I had people who needed it, but I didn't keep any for myself. I didn't want anything from him, even his name. I used Henshaw because it was my mother's maiden name.'

'What's happened to him since? Does he trouble you?'

'He's in jail at the moment, for several years, hopefully. I told you how I took business courses after that, and started on the life I live now.' She raised her wine bottle to the moon. 'Independence every time. Cheers!'

'Independence or isolation?' he asked.

She shrugged. 'Does it matter? Either way, it's better to rely on yourself.'

He sighed. 'I guess so.'

He was glad she couldn't see his face, lest his thoughts showed. He was remembering one night, a lifetime ago, when she'd endured a bad day at work and thrown herself into his arms.

'What would I do without you?' she'd sighed. 'That rotten photographer—goodness, but he's nasty! Never mind. I can put up with anything as long as I know I have you—'

'And you'll always have me,' he'd assured her.

Three weeks later, the disaster had separated them.

'Better rely on yourself,' he repeated, 'rather than on a fool who thought it was funny to conceal his real background, and plunged you both into tragedy.'

'Hey, I wasn't getting at you. Nobody knows what's just around the corner.' She laughed. 'After all, we never saw this coming, did we?'

'And you'd have run a mile if you'd known. I remember you saying so.' He waited for her answer. It didn't come. 'How long ago since your divorce?' he asked.

'About five years. Since then I've been Mrs Henshaw, bestriding the financial world. It suits me. Remember you used to joke about my having a great brain?'

'It wasn't entirely a joke. I think I was a bit jealous of the way you could read something once and remember it like it was set in stone.'

'There now, I told you I was made to be a businesswoman.'

'But that's not your only talent. Why didn't you go back to modelling? You're still beautiful.'

'Not really.'

'I say you are,' he said fiercely.

'I won't argue about it. But it takes more than beauty and I've lost something special. I know that. I knew it then. I'd look in the mirror and see that a light had gone out inside me. Besides,' she hurried on before he could protest, 'I wanted to try something new. It was my choice. Life moves on, we don't stay in the same place.

'Cassie was one person. Mrs Henshaw is another. I became quite pleased with her. She takes people by surprise. Some of them are even scared of her.'

'And you like people being scared of you?'

'Not all the time, but it has its uses. She's a bright lady is Mrs Henshaw. Lots of common sense.'

'Now you're scaring *me*.'

'Good.'

'So I've got to get used to Mrs Henshaw hanging around, when the one I want is Cassie?'

'I'm not sure that's a wise choice. Mrs Henshaw has to get that hotel set up. You need her expertise, her "great brain". Cassie wouldn't be up to the job.'

She managed to say it in a teasing tone, and he managed a smile in reply. But they both knew that she was conveying a subtle warning.

Go slowly. Don't rush it. A false step could mean disaster.

'I think we should go back now,' she said.

She rose and offered him her hand. He hesitated only a moment before nodding and taking it. In this way, with him following her lead, they strolled back to the hotel.

CHAPTER NINE

SHE slept alone that night. Marcel kissed her at the door, touched her face with his fingertips and hurried away. She smiled at his retreating figure, glad that he had the sensitivity not to try to overwhelm her with passion at this moment.

After everything that had happened, all the unexpected revelations, the business of deciding her appearance next morning was a minefield. In the end she selected clothes that were respectable rather than forbidding, and wore her hair drawn back, but not scraped tightly, so that it framed her face softly before vanishing over her shoulders.

When she entered the office he was deep in a phone call, his manner agitated. He waved for her to come in, then turned away. He was talking French but she managed to make out that he was about to go away. The idea didn't seem to please him, for he slammed down the phone and snapped, *'Imbécile! Idiot!'*

'Somebody let you down?' she asked.

'Yes, he's made a mess of a deal I trusted to him, and now I have to go and rescue it. It'll take a few days. Come here!' He hugged her fiercely. 'I don't want to leave you. You should come with me and—'

'No,' she said firmly. 'I'd be a distraction and you've got to keep your mind on business.'

'I'd planned such a day for us. I was going to take you over Paris—'

'Paris will still be here when you get back.' She added significantly, 'And so will I.'

His brow darkened. 'Your word of honour?'

'I told you, I have no reason to leave now.'

Reluctantly he departed, giving her one last anxious look from the door. She saw him go with regret, yet also with a faint twinge of relief. His possessiveness was like a reproach to her. She couldn't blame him for it, but she sensed that it could be a problem, one to which he was blind.

Knowing herself better than Marcel could, she sensed that Mrs Henshaw was more than just an outward change. Her businesslike appearance really did represent a certain reality inside. For the moment Cassie and Mrs Henshaw must live side by side, each one taking the spotlight according to need. But which one of them would finally emerge as her true self? Even she could not be certain about that.

She'd hinted as much to Marcel the previous evening, but she knew he didn't really understand. Or perhaps didn't want to understand. That was the thought that made her a little uneasy.

For the next few days she was Mrs Henshaw, deep in business and thoroughly enjoying herself. Vera introduced her to the chief members of the staff, who had clearly been instructed to cooperate with her. She went through the books and knew she was impressing them with her knowledge of finance.

Then there were the builders who had renovated and extended La Couronne, and who spoke to her at Marcel's command. The more she listened, the more she understood what he'd been trying to do, how well he'd succeeded, and what he wanted in London. Ideas began to flower inside her. She would have much to tell him when he returned on Thursday.

He called her several times a day on the hotel's landline. Wryly she realised that in this way he could check that she was there. Just once he called her cellphone, and that was when she was out shopping. He managed to sound cheerful but she sensed the underlying tension, especially when he said, 'Don't be long getting back to the hotel. There's a lot to do.'

'I'm on my way back now,' she assured him.

Vera greeted her in a flurry of nerves. 'He was very upset when he called and found you not here,' she said.

'Don't worry; he tried my cellphone and I answered at once.' She added reassuringly, 'So when he calls, you can tell him that I'm not slacking on the job.'

Not wanting to embarrass the secretary, whom she liked, she got straight back to work. A few minutes later Vera's phone rang and she shut the door to answer it discreetly.

Poor Marcel, Cassie thought. *I suppose I can't blame him for expecting me to vanish in a puff of smoke. He'll understand, in time.*

By now everyone knew who she was, and the power she possessed, and they would scurry to give her only the best. On Wednesday evening the cook and head waiter joined her at the table for a few minutes, urging her to try new dishes.

They were both attractive men, middle-aged but with appreciative eyes, and they enjoyed talking to her about Paris, which they insisted on calling 'the city of love'.

'You work too hard, *madame,*' the cook told her. 'You should be out there exploring this magical place, becoming imbued with its spirit. Then you would know what to do for the hotel in London.'

'I'm afraid London lacks Paris's air of romance,' she mourned, and they solemnly agreed with her.

Once, long ago, Marcel had whispered in the night, 'I will take you to Paris and show you my city. We will walk the streets together, and you will breathe in the atmosphere of love that is to be found nowhere else.'

'You sound like a guidebook,' she'd complained.

'Actually, I got it out of a guidebook,' he'd admitted sheepishly.

She began to laugh, and he'd joined her. They had clung together, rocking back and forth in bed until the laughter ended in passionate silence, the way everything seemed to end in those days.

He never did take me to Paris, she thought now, sadly. And it would have been so wonderful.

Suddenly he seemed to be there in front of her, laughing joyfully as he'd done in his carefree youth, before cares had fallen on him in a cruel deluge.

'Ah, Monsieur Falcon,' the waiter called. 'How nice to see you back.'

She blinked in disbelief. It wasn't a fantasy. He really was there, standing before her, as though he'd risen from her dreams.

'Good evening,' he said cheerfully. 'I needn't ask if you've missed me. Clearly you haven't.'

'I've been so well looked after that I've barely noticed you were gone,' she teased.

His employees greeted him respectfully before rising from the table and leaving them alone.

'Come with me,' he said, drawing her to her feet.

'But the chef has spent hours preparing—'

'I said come *on.*'

He was laughing but also totally serious, she realised, as she felt herself drawn across the floor and out of the restaurant.

'Where are we going?' she asked breathlessly.

'Wait and see. *Taxi!*'

When they were settled in the back seat she said, 'You weren't supposed to come back until tomorrow.'

'Sorry to disappoint you. Shall I go away again?'

'No, I think I can just about put up with you. Hey, what are you doing?'

'What do you think? Come here.'

'Mmmmmmm!'

Suddenly the boy she'd loved long ago was in her arms again, banishing the severe man he'd become. Eventually that might prove unrealistic, but right now she was too delighted to care about anything else.

Especially being realistic.

'Where are we going?' she asked when she could breathe again.

'Sightseeing. Look.'

Gazing out, she could see that they were driving along the River Seine, with the Eiffel Tower growing closer and closer, until at last they turned over a bridge, heading across the water, straight to the Tower. There they took the elevator up higher and higher, to a restaurant more than four hundred feet above the ground, where he led her to a table by the window.

From here it seemed as if all Paris was laid out for her delight, glittering lights against the darkness, stretching into infinity. She regarded it in awed silence.

'I think it's the most beautiful thing I've ever seen,' she whispered.

'We dreamed of coming here. Do you remember?'

'Oh, yes, I remember.'

She didn't speak for a while, but gazed out, transfixed by the beauty.

'I've always wanted to come to Paris. I kept hoping that the next modelling job would take me there, but I was always unlucky.'

'So now I can show it to you, as I promised.'

'And every girl in Paris will envy me the attention of Marcel Falcon, famous for his harem.'

'Nonsense!'

'It's not.' She chuckled. 'After we met that first night I researched you online, and discovered a lot of interesting things.'

'Don't believe everything you read,' he said wryly.

'Oh, but I'd like to believe it. It was so fascinating. I looked in a web encyclopedia and the entry under "Personal Life" went on for ever. I couldn't keep up. Josie and Leyla, Myra, Ginette and—now, who was the other one? Just let me think.'

'All right,' he growled, 'you've had your fun.'

'After what I read, I don't think you should lecture me about having fun. Tell me about that woman who—'

His scowl stopped her in her tracks. 'Have you finished?' he grunted.

'I've barely started.'

'What would you think of me if I'd had no social life?'

'That you were honest, virtuous, shining white—and the biggest bore in the world. Of course you've had women, lots of them. So you should.'

'Now you sound like my father.'

'I take it that's not a compliment. I only saw him for a moment that night in London, but I thought you seemed tense in his company. Do you dislike him?'

'Sometimes. Sometimes I admire him.'

'Not love him?'

'I don't think he's bothered whether anyone loves him or not. If he was he wouldn't alienate them as he does. All he really cares about is making people do what he wants.' Seeing her wry smile, he ground his teeth, 'OK, fine! Say it.'

'You have been known to want your own way,' she teased.

'And to go about getting it in a way that's—shall we say, cunning and determined?'

'If you mean cheating and bullying, why not say so?'

'I didn't want to insult you. Or would it be a compliment?'

'My father would certainly take it as a compliment. A chip off the old block, that's what he'd call me.'

'Were you at odds with him when you were living in London, that time?'

'I resented him, the person he was, the way he lived, the way he treated people. He seemed to think he could do exactly as he liked, and everyone would just have to put up with it. When I was a child I thought he and my mother were married. They seemed like a normal couple. He wasn't at home very much but I thought that was just because of his work. Then suddenly it all changed. It seemed he'd had a wife in England all the time. At last she'd found out about his other family and divorced him, taking Darius and Jackson.'

Cassie had heard some of this before, from Freya, but Marcel's own view of his colourful childhood had a new significance.

'So then my mother married him and we went to live in England. After a couple of years his first wife died and Darius and Jackson came to live with us.'

'That must have made for a tense situation.'

'It could have been, but Darius and I got on better than you might expect. We were both naturally rebellious and we used to team up against Amos, be co-conspirators, give each other alibis when necessary. I really missed the fun of being wicked together when it was all over.

'Of course the marriage didn't last. He got up to his old tricks and she was expected to put up with it because he was Amos Falcon, a man with enough money to do as he liked.'

'That would be enough to put you off money for life,' she mused.

'That's what I felt, disgust with him and everything he stood for. We found out about his other sons, Travis in America, and Leonid in Russia. I often saw my mother crying, and there were times when I did hate him. I might be his son but I wanted to be as different from him as possible.

'Mama and I came back to Paris and tried to forget him. But he wouldn't let us. He kept turning up on the doorstep. Once his property, always his property. Especially me. I was his son so I was bound to be like him. It was no use telling him that I didn't feel at all like him and didn't want to.'

He made a wry face. 'I guess he knew me better than I knew myself. I fooled around in London, pretending I wasn't connected with him, not using his name, but when the crash came I fled back to my mother in Paris. At first I told myself the future was open, all paths were open to me. I didn't have to take the one that led to Amos.

'But in the end I faced reality. There was only one road, and he stood at the end, waiting for me to admit the truth. I called him in Monte Carlo, where he was living for tax reasons. After that I took lessons in being Amos Falcon.' He assumed a flourishing air. 'I passed them with flying colours.'

'Or you think you did,' she said gently.

'What does that mean?'

'It means I don't think you're as like him as you believe.'

'Maybe. I'm not sure any more. I was certain in those days because I thought he and his way of life was all I had left in the world. Nothing mattered but money, so I went after it because it could fill all the gaping holes.'

'And did it?' she asked.

He shook his head. 'Nothing could. But I wouldn't face it. I told myself it was all your fault. Every bad thing that happened, every cruel disappointment was your fault. That was the only way I—' His hand tightened on his glass.

'Steady, you'll break it,' she said.

'If you only knew—'

'But I do. I had a bad time too, but I don't think I suffered as much as you did. I missed you and grieved for you, but I never had the pain of thinking you'd betrayed me.'

'Didn't you? After what I called you when I saw you at the airport? Didn't I betray you when I tore up that letter?'

'Marcel, stop it,' she said firmly. Taking his hands in hers, she went on, 'You mustn't obsess about that.'

'How can I help it? I could have made it right and I made a mess of everything. I could have spared us ten years of suffering. Why don't you blame me? Why don't you hate me?'

'Would that make you feel better?' she asked softly. 'Shall I beat you up and then say, "Fine, now we're even"?'

'It's what you ought to do.'

'Yes, but I never did do what I ought to do. You said so a hundred times. I never hated you, and if anything good comes out of this it will be that you won't hate me any more.'

'If anything good—? Can you doubt it?'

'I hope for a thousand good things, but we don't know what they are yet.'

'But surely we—?'

'We have to be patient. We're strangers to each other now.'

'You'll never be a stranger to me.'

'That's lovely, but it isn't true. It can't be. We know the people we used to be, but not the people we are now. We have to discover each other again before—'

'Before we can love each other? Don't you want us to?'

Before the intensity of his eyes she looked away. 'I don't know,' she admitted. 'It frightens me. I guess I'm just easily scared these days.' She clasped his hands again. 'I need a friend.'

'Friend,' he echoed, as though trying to believe what he'd heard.

'Someone who understands things that nobody else in the

world understands. Please, Marcel, be my friend. Be that first, and then maybe—if we're patient—and lucky—'

'You know what you're telling me, don't you? You can't love me and you don't want me to love you.'

'No!' she said fiercely. 'It isn't that. But I'm scared. Aren't you?'

'I wasn't before. I am now. I thought the other night—'

'The other night we found each other again, but only in one way. And—' she gave a reminiscent smile '—it was so lovely.'

'But not enough,' he said.

'Would it be enough for you, always? Won't there come a time when you're lying in my arms wondering if you can really trust me?'

He didn't answer, and she followed his thoughts. She'd hit a nerve, leaving him shocked and appalled at himself. He'd had as much as he could stand, she decided, and she must bring this to an end.

'I want to look at the view again,' she said, rising and going to the window. 'I've never seen such beauty.'

He made a suitable reply, and they left the dangerous subject behind. For the rest of the evening they kept carefully to indifferent subjects, presenting the appearance of a conventional couple, with no sign of the turbulence whirling inside them.

She knew that she must face the fact that there was a sad but crucial difference between them. With the truth finally revealed he'd become open to her, as though he was hers again. It was she who was holding back.

The feeling of detachment was painful. She longed to throw open her arms in welcome, vowing that everything was good again and all suffering would be forgotten. But the lessons of the past few years couldn't simply be unlearned. Most piercing of all was the fear of hurting him again.

Returning to the hotel, he saw her to her door but, to her relief, didn't try to come in. He'd read the signal she'd sent him and accepted it, however reluctantly. He would give her time, but his eyes told of his turmoil.

'I'll see you tomorrow, then,' he said. 'There are some figures we must go through. Goodnight.'

'Goodnight,' she whispered.

He touched her cheek, then departed quickly.

He had to be away several times in the next couple of weeks. When he returned they would dine together and talk, just as she'd hoped. On those evenings he kept his distance both physically and emotionally, making her wonder if he was following her lead or if he'd really decided against her. That thought filled her with irrational dismay.

You're mad, she told herself. *You don't know what you want.*

Which was true.

One afternoon, working together in his apartment, they had a bickering disagreement which threatened to turn into a quarrel. Afterwards she could never remember exactly what it had been about. Or if it had been about anything except the fact that a final separation might be looming.

'I should never have taken this job,' she sighed. 'Let's end it now. I'll go back to England and we need never see or think of each other again.'

'Do you imagine I'll allow that?'

'I don't think you could stop me leaving.'

'I could stop you any time I want to. You won't leave me, Cassie. I won't stand for it.'

'Don't,' she said harshly. 'That's the sort of thing Jake used to say. I can't bear it when you talk like him.'

He stared. 'Do I talk like him very often?'

'Sometimes. He regarded me as bought and paid for, and he made it plain.'

'And you think that's how I see you?'

'No, I—'

'Can't you understand that I still dread the thought of waking up to find you not there? I try to tell myself to be sensible but in that great echoing vacuum there's no sense, only horror. Every time you leave the room there's a voice in my head that says you won't come back. You fill my dreams but you also fill my nightmares.'

'Then perhaps you should let me go, and never think of me again.'

'And know that you'll never think of *me* again? That's the biggest nightmare of all. Sometimes I wish I had the strength to let you go, because then I might find peace. Not happiness, but peace. But I can't do it.'

She nodded. 'I know,' she said huskily. 'Me too.'

Now, she thought hopefully, they could talk and rediscover each other in yet another way. The road lay open before them.

But he seemed reluctant to take it, turning back to the computer screen.

Never mind, she thought. The chance would come again.

Next day Marcel announced that they needed to spend a few days in London.

'My purchase of the hotel isn't finalised yet and I'm getting impatient, so let's see if we can put some rockets under people. Vera, we'll need train tickets.'

'Train tickets?' his secretary echoed.

'That's what I said,' he called over his shoulder as he left the room.

'First time I've ever known him not take a plane,' Vera mused. 'I wonder why.'

Cassie thought she knew why and her heart was warmed by his concern for her, although when she tried to thank him he loftily brushed the matter aside as 'Pure convenience.'

'Of course,' she said, and kissed him.

This was the side of him she had loved, and for which she could feel the love creeping back. That might be dangerous while she was still unsure who this new man was, and how much of his old self still existed. But right now she was happy to take the risk.

Rather than leave it to Vera, she volunteered to book their hotel rooms.

'At the Crown Hotel,' she announced.

'Not The Crown yet,' Marcel pointed out. 'Until I sign the final papers it's still The Alton.'

'To them it's The Alton, to us it's The Crown,' she declared triumphantly. 'Everything's going to go right, and nothing will go wrong.'

'Yes,' he said with a smile that touched her heart. 'Nothing will go wrong. We won't let it.'

But he frowned when he saw the bookings she'd made.

'Separate rooms? Surely we could be together?'

'You're going to be the big boss. We need to preserve your dignity,' she said.

'If that means Mrs Henshaw in steel spectacles, forget it. I don't like that woman.'

'Then why did you hire her?'

'Because she didn't fool me. I want the real woman, the one she hides inside.'

'Unfortunately,' she murmured, 'it's Mrs Henshaw who's good with figures.'

He seemed struck by this. 'Ah, yes! Problem!'

Then someone came into the room and it could be passed off as a joke. But it lingered in her mind as a warning that troubles might lie ahead.

When they arrived in London Mrs Henshaw was at her most efficient, ironing out last minute problems, talking with bank managers and accountants. Marcel dominated the meetings, but whenever she spoke he listened intently, even admiringly. But afterwards he observed, to nobody in particular, 'I shall be glad when this is all over.'

There was an infuriating delay in the finance, owing to the bank demanding extra guarantees.

'Is this going to make it impossible?' she asked, seeing him gloomy.

'No, I can manage it, one way or another. I just don't want to have to ask my father's help. His fingers are in too many pies already.' He gave a slight shudder. 'Now come on, let's have some dinner.'

'Yes, let's see if I can cheer you up.'

'*You* can't,' he said, eyeing her 'Mrs Henshaw' appearance. 'But *she* could.'

'Mmm, I'll see if she's free tonight.'

'She'd better be.'

She wore her hair long, tumbling over her shoulders, and when they met for dinner in the restaurant he nodded approval.

'Will I pass?' she teased.

'You will, but we can't go on like this. It's like living with Jekyll and Hyde.'

'Really? So am I Dr Jekyll, middle-aged, scientific, brainy and kind? Or am I Mr Hyde, young and cruel?'

He sipped his wine for a moment before saying, 'Joking apart, it's more subtle than that. With Jekyll and Hyde you could always tell from the appearance. But with you I can't always tell. Whichever one you look like, the other one is always likely to pop out for a few moments, then dash back.'

'Yes, we exist side by side,' she agreed. 'Which may be confusing.'

'*May* be?'

'But why worry if ditzy Cassie sometimes has a great brain? There was a time when you knew that.'

'I know, I know. In those days—the great brain was just a part of you. I never dreamed it would take over your whole life in the form of Mrs Henshaw!'

'I know. But Mrs Henshaw was always there, lurking.'

'Yes, lurking, but now she's pounced. She's a bit alarming.'

'Maybe she wouldn't be if you knew her better,' she said, smiling.

This was the tone of the rest of the evening, light, easy, full of merriment and goodwill. She was happy, although still disturbed by a feeling that was half hope, half caution.

On the one hand there was the thoughtfulness that had made Marcel take the train for her sake. On the other hand was his reluctance to accept Mrs Henshaw as part of who she was. But that would sort itself out soon, she reassured herself.

In the meantime she was feeling exhausted. She'd worked through most of last night and all today, determined to stay on top of her duties. Now she would have given much to be able to sleep.

Hoping to liven herself up a little she took an extra glass of wine, and knew fairly soon that she'd made a mistake. If anything, she was woozier than before.

'I think I'll have an early night,' she said, and he rose at once, giving her his arm.

He followed her into her room and turned her towards him, looking down at her face with a questioning look. 'Are you all right?'

'Yes, just tired.'

'I'll say goodnight then.' He lifted her chin and laid his lips gently against hers.

Her head swam. The last time they had kissed there had been an edge of hostility, even violence, on her side as well as his. But now his touch was gentle, reminding her of happier times, and she responded with pleasure, although its edge was blunted by drowsiness.

'Cassie,' he murmured, 'Cassie…don't shut me out… please…'

'I don't…mean to…'

'Kiss me—I've waited for this so long and now…kiss me…'

She could feel the softness of the bed beneath her, his fingers opening her dress. Deep inside she sensed her own response, but waves of sleep washed over her brain.

Now, she thought, he would take what he pleased, knowing she was beyond resistance. She hadn't wanted it this way. Their next love-making should have been a union of hearts as well as bodies—not like this.

'Cassie—Cassie—*Cassie?*'

She opened her eyes, whispering, 'Marcel.'

His face was full of sudden suspicion. 'Are you entirely sober?'

'I…don't think so. I shouldn't have…oh. dear.'

His face tensed. He drew back and looked down at where her breasts were partially exposed, showing all the lushness that he'd always enjoyed. For a brief moment he let his fingertips linger on the swell, relishing the silky skin. His head drooped and she waited for the feel of his lips. But then he stiffened as though a bolt of lightning had gone through him. Next moment he'd practically hurled himself off the bed.

'Marcel—' she whispered.

He was breathing hard. 'Goodnight.'

He yanked at the duvet and threw it over her so that he could no longer see the glorious temptation, and moved towards the door.

'You're going?' she asked vaguely.

'Of course I'm going,' he answered. 'You really think I'm

going to—when you don't really know what you're doing? A
fine opinion you have of me. Goodnight.'

'Marcel—'

The door slammed. There followed the noise of his footsteps running down the corridor, but she never heard them.
She was already asleep.

CHAPTER TEN

NEXT morning he greeted her briskly. 'Just one more day and then we can be gone. There's some papers over there that need—' He couldn't meet her eyes.

It was almost funny, she thought. Last night he'd behaved like a perfect gentleman, refusing to take advantage of her vulnerability. It was practically worth a medal for chivalry. And he was secretly ashamed of it.

Which was a pity, because she couldn't tell him how proud she was of his generosity.

That evening they were invited to a business dinner, where networking would be a high priority.

'And I promise not to touch anything stronger than orange juice,' she said.

'And then—?'

'And then I'll be fully awake and alert, and I'll know exactly what I'm doing.'

She gave him a quick kiss and vanished, leaving him staring at her door in frustration, admiration and bemusement.

In her preparations, Cassie and Mrs Henshaw came together, the dress with a mysterious combination of severity and temptation, the hair drawn lightly back, but not scraped. She was a huge success. It was Marcel who had a lacklustre evening, unable to take his eyes off her and letting business opportunities slip by.

Later, as they approached his suite, she pulled her hair free, shaking it so that it flowed over her shoulders and forward down her breasts.

'You should be careful,' he murmured. 'A conceited man might interpret that as a hint.'

'Better a conceited man than a slow-witted one,' she said, slipping her arms around his neck. 'Just when will you get the message?'

'Right now,' he said, clasping her with one hand and pushing the door open with the other.

Twice since their meeting they had shared passion. The first time had been in anger, the second time the feeling had been gentler, but still tense.

But now they rediscovered many things they had both thought lost for ever. His touch brought her only delight, the look in his eyes raised her to the heights. He loved her slowly, prolonging every moment so that she could feel his tenderness.

And something else, perhaps. Love? Did she dare to hope?

When he finally abandoned control and yielded to her completely she held him close, hoping and praying for the miracle.

At last he whispered, 'Is everything all right?'

'Yes,' she said slowly. 'Very much all right.'

In the next few hours they loved, slept, and loved again. Now she was filled with deep joy, sensing the approaching moment when all would be made well.

Next day they returned to Paris and plunged back into work, both content to do so, knowing that better times were coming.

Soon, she promised herself, she would say the words that would make everything different between them. But first she would enjoy the pleasure that only he could give her. There would be plenty of time for talk.

He didn't even ask if he could come to her room. Now he knew he didn't need to ask. Nestled down in bed, they found themselves and each other again and again, before sleeping in utter contentment.

She awoke to find him watching her, and made a decision.

'Marcel—'

'Yes, Cassie?'

She took a deep breath. All hesitation gone. What better time could there ever be?

But before she could speak his cellphone shrilled.

He swore and grappled for it in his clothes. Cassie closed her eyes and groaned.

'Yes?' he answered. Then his face changed and he grew alert. 'Freya! What's the matter? You sound upset—all right, calm down. How can I help? What?—What's got into the old man now?—I don't believe it, even of him.'

At last he hung up and flung her a despairing glance.

'My father's up to his tricks again. He's on his way here. I think he's beginning to realise that he's not going to marry her off to Darius so he's turning his fire on me.'

Groaning, she covered her eyes with her hands. Of all the times for this to happen! Now she couldn't say what she'd meant to. For the moment the spell was broken.

'I need your help,' Marcel continued. 'So does Freya. If there's one thing she doesn't want it's to be stuck with me.'

Cassie forced herself to concentrate. 'Well, Freya was very kind to me, so I'll do all I can to save her from that terrible fate. Just tell me what to do.'

'When we take them to dinner we must act like a couple, just until he gets the message.'

'When are they going to arrive here?'

'Soon. Let's hurry.'

He was out of bed, throwing on his clothes. She sighed

and followed suit. The time would come, she promised herself. But she must be patient for a while.

Amos and Freya arrived two hours later. When Marcel had shown them to their rooms Amos said, 'I thought you'd still be in London working on that new place. But I dare say the admirable Mrs Henshaw is taking care of everything.'

'Admirable certainly,' Marcel agreed. 'In fact I've brought her here to study La Couronne so that she'll have a more precise idea of my wishes. She's looking forward to meeting you again when we all have dinner tonight.'

Amos made a displeased face. 'No need to invite her to dinner. I'm not in the mood for business.'

'But I'm in the mood to meet Mrs Henshaw again,' Freya said quickly. 'I liked her so much when we met in England.'

'She's eager to see you too,' Marcel assured her. 'Why don't you go up to the office and talk to her?'

The meeting between the two women was friendly and eager. Cassie had pleasant memories of Freya's kindly attention when she'd banged her head, but she'd been too confused to notice much about her. Now she saw an attractive young woman in her late twenties, slim and vigorous, with light brown hair that was almost auburn, green eyes and a cheeky smile. She ordered tea for them both and they settled down comfortably.

'I'm so glad you took the job with Marcel,' Freya said. 'He was so afraid that you wouldn't.'

'He thought I'd refuse it?'

'I don't know, but he seemed very worried about it. He must have heard a lot about your business skills.'

'Yes, I guess it must have been that,' Cassie murmured.

'He says you're having dinner with us. I'm so glad.'

Her fervent tone prompted Cassie to say cautiously, 'I gather Mr Falcon is trying to throw the two of you together.'

'Sort of. I don't think he's quite given up hope of Darius, but—'

'But he's keeping all his options open,' Cassie supplied. 'Just what you'd expect an entrepreneur to do.'

'Yes. Do you know what they're talking about now, why Amos originally came here? Bringing me was just an afterthought. He's helping Marcel raise extra funds for the London hotel. Somebody owes him money and there's a loophole in the contract by which Amos can get repaid earlier. So he's twisting the poor fellow's arm.'

'Not a nice man,' Cassie agreed.

'He's always thought Darius was that way inclined too. And Marcel is next in the money-making stakes. Honestly, who'd want to marry a man like that?'

'Nobody in their right mind,' Cassie agreed.

The phone rang. It was Marcel, wanting Vera, but the secretary had just left.

'I need some papers. Can you bring them to me? You'll find them—'

'No problem,' she said when he'd explained. 'I'll be right down with them.'

Approaching Amos's room, she could hear raised voices. One of them was Amos, but the loudest belonged to a young man who seemed almost hysterical.

'But it isn't fair. Can't you see that?'

'It's in the contract.' That was Amos.

'But you said it was just a fallback, and you'd never make use of it—'

'I said I probably wouldn't make use of it. It wasn't a guarantee.'

'You made it sound like one—as long as I kept up the repayments—'

'Which have sometimes been late.'

'They're up-to-date at this moment. Surely that's what counts?'

'*I* say what counts.' Amos's voice was as harsh as sandpaper, and Cassie stepped back from the door in revulsion.

The next moment she was glad of it for the door was yanked open by a man who came flying out. He turned to scream back, 'Be damned to you! I hope you rot in hell!'

Then he dashed off, forcing her to flatten herself against the wall. She stayed there, breathing out, trying to calm down. But before she was ready to enter the room she heard Marcel's voice.

'There was no need to go quite so far.'

'Don't give me that. I know just how far to go. I didn't get where I am by weakening. Nor should you.'

'I don't. I can be tough when I have to, but it's a new age. Subtlety can be better.'

'Only one thing matters,' came Amos's rasping voice. 'Does he have the cash or doesn't he?'

'According to him he doesn't. It might not be wise to press him too far.'

'Give me patience! Will nothing cure you of the habit of believing what people say?'

'It can actually be useful sometimes.'

'Not this time. Leave that man for me to deal with.'

Cassie backed away, wishing she could run far away from this horrible conversation that exhibited all the worst of Amos Falcon. She was glad that Marcel had had the decency to argue against him, although she wished he'd done so more strongly.

He'd advised his father to soften his stance, not out of kindness, but because subtlety offered a better chance of a profit. It was only a different road to the same money-filled destination.

Suddenly she was glad that she hadn't opened her heart to him that morning.

Amos Falcon was exactly as Cassie remembered him from their brief earlier meeting—in his seventies, heavily built with a harsh face and piercing eyes. He smiled a lot and his words were often cordial, but his eyes were cold.

He greeted her politely at dinner that evening and indicated a chair next to himself. Since the table was oblong, this effectively separated them from Marcel and Freya, sitting on the other side.

As so often these days, her appearance was a subtle combination of the two women who seemed to inhabit her. Amos regarded her with admiration.

'I'm going to enjoy talking to you this evening. Marcel, you entertain Freya. I want to get to know Mrs Henshaw.'

He proceeded to give Cassie all his attention, asking about her career, her abilities, the recent trip to England.

'Don't know why problems are cropping up now,' he growled. 'Those damned banks!'

'Well, I suppose they—' Cassie began.

She continued in this way for a while, talking generally without giving away any information about Marcel's dealings. Amos listened, nodding sometimes, and in this way the meal passed.

Over coffee things changed. Marcel joined in and the talk became all business. Amos mentioned the man who'd been there earlier, refusing to hand over money.

'He'll see sense,' he said. 'I'll make sure of that. He thinks he can defy me and get away with it. The best way—'

The two women met each other's eyes.

'You two don't need us for this kind of talk,' Freya said. 'Shall we—?'

'Yes, let's,' Cassie said, rising and following her. 'Goodnight, gentlemen.'

They said goodnight and returned at once to their discussion.

'They hardly noticed us go,' Freya said as they went up in the elevator, and Cassie nodded.

Upstairs in Cassie's rooms, Freya threw herself into an armchair with a sigh of relief. 'Oh, thank heavens!' she said. 'I'd had as much as I could stand.' She gave a laugh. 'Of course you probably find it interesting. Sorry, I forgot about that.'

'No, I was just as glad to get away,' Cassie said. 'I don't like it when it gets brutal.'

'Me too. I much prefer a good TV show and a handsome man. Hey, look at him!'

She'd flicked on the set, and suddenly the screen was filled with a staggeringly handsome young man.

'Know who that is?' she asked.

'Yes, it's Marcel's half-brother, Travis,' Cassie said. 'They started showing *The Man From Heaven* a few weeks ago, and I've been watching it because of Marcel. Who was his mother? Another of Amos's wives?'

'No, she was an American girl he met while he was over there on business.'

'So if he can't marry you to Darius or Marcel, Travis is the next in line?' Cassie asked, amused.

'Either him or Leonid, who lives in Russia, and who nobody seems to meet. Or Jackson, the naturalist. I'd have to be crazy to marry any of them, but especially Travis. His wife would never have a moment's peace he's so handsome. Mind you, it would be much the same with Marcel, who's also very handsome.'

'Is he?' Cassie asked indifferently.

'Well, some women think so. Is that tea? Thank you, I could do with it. Sometimes I think Amos insists on champagne all the time as a kind of status symbol, just to underline how far he's come from his days of poverty, when actually I'm dying for a cuppa.'

They sipped their tea in deep contentment.

'Why do you put up with it?' Cassie asked. 'Can't you escape him?'

'Yes, soon, hopefully. I'd like to go back to working as a nurse. The high life doesn't really suit me. I suppose I shouldn't complain. He's decent to my mother, and good to me. He wants me in the family.'

'I suppose that's nice of him.'

'Ye-es,' Freya said, unconvinced. 'It's only because he's never had a daughter and he sees a chance of "completing the set". A sharp businessman covers every angle.'

'That's true.'

'A few months ago Amos had a scare with his heart. He's too stubborn to admit that it might be serious so my mother asked me to come and stay with them for a while. This way he always has a nurse on hand, but he can pretend I'm just visiting.

'All his sons came to see him, just in case it was the last time. From things he said, I know he wanted to take a good look at them and decide which one was really his true heir. Whichever one he decides on will get an extra share of his fortune. And whichever one marries me will get an extra dose of money too, as a reward for "doing what Daddy wants".'

'Oh, heavens!' Cassie exclaimed in horror. 'How do you put up with it?'

'Because basically I'm free. I can walk out and get a job elsewhere any time I want. He got me on this trip by staging a dizzy spell at the last moment, so I came with him to keep my mother happy. But that's it! From now on I'm going to reclaim my life.'

A sense of mischief made Cassie say, 'Amos is a man very used to getting his own way. You might yet end up as his daughter-in-law.'

'I suppose anything's possible, however unlikely. But it won't be Darius because I think he's going to make it work with Harriet, the young woman he brought to the wedding in London. And it won't be Marcel. He wouldn't suit me at all.'

'You sound very sure,' Cassie said, not looking at her. 'Why is that?'

'He just sees things in black and white all the time. Where brains are concerned he's as sharp as they come. But emotionally I think he imagines things are more straightforward than they ever really are. Maybe that's because he doesn't seem to have much emotional life.'

'Doesn't he? Let me pour you some more tea.'

'I don't think so. Women galore but no real involvement. And if that's what satisfies him, he's not for me. And he won't marry for Amos's money because he doesn't need it. Sometimes I think he's just that little bit too much like Amos.'

'Or maybe he just likes to believe that things can work out simply and straightforwardly,' Cassie mused.

'True. Actually, I think a lot of men are like that—just not geared up to see how complicated life can be.'

'Yes,' Cassie said quietly. 'That's it.'

'Oh well, let them get on with it.'

Freya gave a theatrical shudder and glanced back at the screen where the drama series was still showing. Travis's face was still there.

'Why is this show called *The Man From Heaven*?' she queried.

'I think he's supposed to be at least partly an angel,' Cassie said.

'No guy as good-looking as that was ever an angel. But hey, don't you dare tell Amos I said that. I'd get no peace afterwards.'

Cassie chuckled and they continued the evening in perfect accord. She was beginning to feel that Freya was exactly the kind of person she would like to have as a close friend.

But she couldn't guess the astonishing way in which that would one day become true.

It was a couple of weeks later that she opened Marcel's door, stopped on the threshold, then prepared to back off, saying, 'I'm sorry, I didn't know you had someone here.'

'Come in, Mrs Henshaw,' Marcel called cheerfully. 'This is my brother, Darius.'

She'd recognised him from her research of the Falcon family, and knew part of his history. Eldest son of Amos Falcon and a skilled entrepreneur in his own right. Like many others, he'd been hit by the credit crunch and was now the owner of Herringdean, an island that a debtor had dumped on him by way of repayment.

'Darius has just invited me to his wedding,' Marcel explained now. 'He's finally persuaded Harriet to put up with him.'

'It wasn't easy.' Darius grinned. 'She's part of the lifeboat crew on Herringdean and she saved me from drowning in the first few days. Now I never feel safe if she's not around.' He thumped Marcel's shoulder. 'You've got to come. The other lads are all going to be there.'

'Yes, you have brothers all over the world,' Cassie said. 'I remember Freya telling me.'

'That's right, Jackson's going to get a few days off from interviewing animals. I had to twist his arm for that because he finds ferrets more interesting than people. Leonid's going to drop whatever he's doing in Russia and come on over, and the man from heaven has promised to put in an appearance.'

'Ah, yes, I've been watching that on television,' she said, smiling.

'So Travis will be there for the wedding, and so will Marcel. Come on Marcel, say you will.'

'Oh, no. I'm avoiding Amos at the moment. Now he can't marry you to Freya I'm in danger.'

'Dad probably won't be there. He's that mad at me for marrying Harriet that he's snubbing our wedding.'

'Yes and, knowing him, he'll drop in at the last minute,' Marcel observed.

'Coward,' Darius said amiably.

'No, I'll be there, but I want some protection. Mrs Henshaw must come with me and if Dad starts any funny business she'll deal with it.'

'That's the spirit,' Darius said. 'Mrs Henshaw, are you up to the job?'

'I think so,' she said cheerfully. 'If Mr Falcon tries to speak to Marcel I just tell him he must make an appointment through me first.'

'Hey, she's good.' Darius grinned. 'I'll leave you in safe hands. The wedding is next week. I know it's short notice but I can't risk Harriet changing her mind. Besides, she's got this dog—lovely fellow called Phantom. He did a lot to bring us together but he's very old and we want to marry while he's alive to see it.'

'It's not like you to be sentimental,' Marcel said.

'It's not like me to do a lot of things I'm doing these days. But Harriet…well… I don't know how to describe her…she's "the one"…no, that's not it. Well, yes, it is, but it's much more…at least…'

'You're stammering,' Marcel observed.

Darius gave an awkward laugh. 'I guess I am. It's the effect she has on me. She kept her distance for a while because she thought I only wanted to marry her for the sake of the children. I had to…persuade her otherwise.'

'Now you're blushing,' Marcel accused him. 'You, the man I've always admired because he could make everyone scramble to please him, you're scrambling to please Harriet.'

'Yes, I am,' Darius said with a touch of belligerence. 'I've finally got my priorities right, and she's what matters. I know you think I'm making a fool of myself, but I don't care what anyone else thinks. When you find the one, grab her, or you'll regret it all your life.'

'But that's assuming that you find the one in the first place,' Mrs Henshaw pointed out with a friendly smile.

'True. Marcel will probably never find her. Too busy playing the field. Never could commit himself. Probably never will now. Right, I must be off. Here's the details.' He gave her a sheet of paper. 'Get him there on time, see that he behaves.'

'That won't be easy,' she joked. 'But I'll do my best.'

When Darius had gone Marcel said, 'We need to go to London for a few more days to sort out some final details. Then we'll go on to Herringdean in time for the wedding.' He added significantly, 'I'm looking forward to that.'

In the atmosphere of a wedding anything might happen. Answers could be found, love might flower. His eyes told her that he was thinking the same thing.

He began to reach for her, but suddenly her cellphone rang. She answered it, then tensed, growing so still and silent that Marcel was alarmed.

'Don't hang up,' said a man's voice at the other end. 'You know who this is.'

Without replying, she ended the call.

'What's the matter?' Marcel asked, concerned. 'Why are you looking like that? Who was it?'

'Jake,' she said. 'I don't know how he got my number. He must be out of prison. How dare he contact me again!'

'Don't worry; I'll keep you safe,' he promised. 'I won't let him get to you again.'

She longed to believe him, but Jake could always get to her because he never really left her. That was the cruel truth that poisoned her life. Even now he must have been keeping tabs on her to have discovered her new phone number.

It rang again. She answered, saying sharply, 'I'm shutting this down—'

'I'm dying,' Jake said.

'What?'

'I've only got a few days left. I want to see you, Cassie—one last time.'

'*No!*'

'I'm not in prison any more. They let me out to die in hospital. You know the place—'

He gave her the name, while she clenched her free hand, whispering, 'No...no...no...'

'Please—I beg you—'

'No. Understand me, Jake, I don't care if you are dying. I don't want to see you again, ever.'

'Dying?' Marcel echoed.

'He wants me to go and see him.'

'Then tell him you'll go.'

'*What?*'

'I'll take you. You won't be alone.'

'Are you mad?'

'No, I want you to find closure, and this may be the only way you can do it. See him, Cassie. Tie up the ends. Then tell him from both of us to go to hell.'

She stared at him, mesmerised by something fierce and desperate in his voice. This mattered to Marcel. It was there in the tension of his body and the sharp edge of his voice.

'Tell him,' he said. 'Say you'll do it. Say it!'

'Marcel—'

'Say it!'

'Jake,' she said slowly, 'I'm on my way.'

CHAPTER ELEVEN

This time they took the plane to London. On the flight Marcel held her hand in his. She gave him a brief wan smile, but mostly she stared out of the window.

To see Jake again. To be forced back into his company. This was the stuff of nightmares, yet the road was taking her inexorably there and she had no chance of escape.

At last she turned to Marcel, trying to read his expression.

'Why are you doing this?' she murmured. 'It's not just for me, is it?'

'No,' he conceded. 'I need to see him myself. Can you understand that?'

'Yes, I suppose I can understand, but I'm afraid, Marcel.'

'Don't be. I'm here.'

The thought, *Not afraid of him—afraid of you*, winged its way through her mind and vanished into the distance. She didn't really know what she meant by it, and there was no way she could have told him, even if she had known.

She realised that Marcel was pursuing some goal of his own, and she was only part of it. He was like a man who'd travelled on an epic journey and who saw the end in sight.

'I heard you ask how he got your number,' he said. 'Do you think he's been keeping tabs on you?'

'He must have been. Even in prison he's had people on the outside taking his orders. When we were together he had a horrible obsession with me. All he saw was that I was his property. We'd go out to dinner and he'd flaunt me—that's the only word for it. And I'd have to smile and look proud, knowing that as soon as we got home he'd grab me and—'

'Don't!' Marcel said with soft violence. 'Don't.'

He threw himself back in his seat, his eyes closed.

'I'm sorry,' he said at last. 'I can't bear to hear it, but you had to live through it. You must despise me. I don't blame you.'

'We're past that,' she said gently. 'Neither of us knows what it was really like for the other. Let's take it carefully.'

He nodded and they held each other for a few moments.

'Talk to me,' he said at last. 'Tell me anything you like. I want to be part of your life, even that stage of it.'

She sighed. 'There was one moment when I hoped life might not be completely wretched. I was pregnant.'

'You've had a child?' he asked, startled.

'No, I miscarried. That was when Jake went sleeping around. I didn't mind. The less I saw of him, the better. And it gave me a way of divorcing him. He fought me but I had one big weapon.'

'Yes, you must have known a lot of his dark secrets by then.'

'I did, but that wasn't it. The real weapon was the fact that I didn't care about anything. He defeated people by scaring them, and when he knew I couldn't be scared he was left floundering.

'The last thing he said to me was, "You think you've got away from me, but you haven't really." And he was right. Once I'd escaped him all the feelings he'd killed began to come back, and I started caring again. He was always there in my nightmares, and I haven't been able to banish him.'

'But things are different now,' Marcel said firmly. 'We'll defeat him together.' Seeing the confused look in her eyes, he put his hands on either side of her face. 'We will. I promise you.'

'Will we?' she mused. 'Perhaps.'

'You don't believe me, do you? *Do you?*'

'I want to,' she said desperately. 'You don't know how much I want to believe that all the problems could be swept away so simply, but oh, my darling, it's more complicated than that, more worrying, more frightening.'

'But we're together now. How can we be frightened, either of us, while we have each other? We're going to defeat Jake, I promise you.'

She longed to believe him. She didn't have the words to tell him how confused and bewildering was the universe in which they lived now. He'd always seen things in simple black and white, she remembered. And sometimes he'd been right. If only he could be right now. But she was full of apprehension.

They were beginning the descent, and there was no chance to say more.

They had booked a hotel near Heathrow Airport, and after checking in they went straight to the hospital where Jake was living out his last few days.

They found him in a private ward. A guard was sitting by the bed, but he moved discreetly away.

Marcel had kept a firm, comforting grip on her hand, but then he released her and backed into the shadows.

She barely recognised Jake. Once a big, beefy man, he was now skeletally thin.

'Cassie?' he croaked. 'Is that you? I can't see you properly.'

'Yes, it's me.'

'Come closer.'

Reluctantly she leaned down and he reached up a hand to touch her cheek. With an effort she stopped herself from flinching and sat on the bed. He managed a ghastly travesty of a smile, croaking, 'You're still beautiful, still my Cassie.'

'I was never your Cassie,' she said at once.

'You were my wife.'

'Not in my heart. Never.'

'But you're here,' he gasped. 'I knew you'd come.'

'No,' she said quietly. 'Don't fool yourself, Jake. I'm sorry for you, but there's nothing between us. There never was.'

'Oh, you always played hard to get. That's what I loved about you. Yes, we belonged together. I always knew it.'

'And you deluded yourself,' she said, filled with disgust. 'You hurt the man I loved and I stayed with you to protect him. That's the only reason.'

'Him? Don't make me laugh. He was nobody. By now he's probably scraping a living sweeping the streets.'

This was Marcel's moment and he took it, moving out of the shadows to stand beside Cassie.

'You were wrong about that,' he said, 'as you have been wrong about everything.'

'Who the hell are you?' Jake demanded.

'You don't know me? No, I suppose you wouldn't. You got someone else to do your dirty work. They left me lying in a pool of blood in the street. But here I am and now I've seen all I needed to.'

Then Jake did something that astounded them both. He began to laugh.

'Fine talk,' he gasped. 'You think you've won, don't you? If you'd *won* back *then* you would have won. She was young and glorious, better than she'll ever be again in her life. Those were her best years, and they were mine, d'you hear? Mine. I had things you'll never know.'

'No, he had things *you* never knew,' Cassie said. 'He had my love, given freely. That's something you never had.'

Jake barely heard her. His hate-filled eyes were on Marcel.

'You didn't win,' he spat, 'and one day you'll realise that. Cassie died years ago. All you've got now is the shell. You think you have a future? What kind of future? No children. She can't have any.'

'Not with you, maybe,' Marcel said softly.

Jake turned to Cassie and he was suddenly shaken with a coughing fit. His hands gripped her arms with the last of his strength. She hated him but a feeling of pity made her clasp him back.

'You came to me,' he choked. 'You came…you couldn't stay away…'

'I came because he asked me to,' she said with a fierce glance at Marcel. 'Nothing else would have brought me here.'

'You're lying…I'm your husband…Cassie…my Cassie… mine…'

Gasps tore him, growing faster, noisier, until at last he fell back against the pillows.

'You were always mine,' he murmured as his eyes closed.

'No,' she breathed. 'Never, *never!*'

He could no longer hear her. His eyes, half open, stared unseeingly into a hidden distance. His rigid hands, clasping her arms, held her prisoner.

'No,' she wept. 'Please, no.'

In a flash Marcel was there, wrenching Jake's hands away, setting her free.

'Let's go,' he said.

In the taxi he held her shuddering body.

'Everything's all right,' he said. 'It's over now.'

But it wasn't over. And suddenly she doubted that everything would ever be all right.

Back in the hotel he came to her room and immediately called Room Service to order supper. While they waited he went to his own room, returning with his night clothes. When the food arrived he prepared to serve her.

'I'm not really hungry,' she sighed.

'I know, but you have to eat anyway. Don't argue.'

His tone was gentle but firm, and she let him take over. She felt drained and defeated. Where was the sense of triumph that should have filled her? Nothing. Only the troubling sense that Jake had mysteriously won again.

He helped her to undress, then he put her to bed and got in beside her, taking her into his arms, holding her as though in this way he could keep her safe. She snuggled against him, reaching out for that safety.

She fell into a contented sleep and awoke to find him touching her intimately. She responded, giving and seeking love, letting him take her into the dream.

'It's all right,' Marcel murmured. 'He's gone. Now it's just us.'

'Yes,' she said, trying to believe that this was really so.

But there was still a dark and worrying cloud hanging over her. She didn't look at it too closely. She didn't want to understand it.

But some kind of understanding was forced on her when she awoke in the early hours with a headache. Moving quietly not to wake Marcel, she slipped out of bed, and went to her bag, seeking a pill. Not finding what she wanted, she reached her fingers into a small pocket inside that normally she never used. What she found there almost made her heart stop.

Drawing the tiny object out into the light, she surveyed it with horror. It was the ring Jake had given her long ago, and which she'd flung back at him during the divorce.

She remembered how she'd sat by his bed that afternoon, leaning over him, the bag lying on the coverlet. He must have slipped the ring inside when his hand moved towards her. It had fallen into the pocket without her noticing.

With a horrified, sick feeling she realised that it was what he'd always meant to do. By returning it he'd reasserted his claim on her from beyond the grave.

'Cassie?' Marcel appeared, rubbing sleep from his eyes. 'Are you all right?'

'Yes, fine,' she said, closing the bag. 'I'm just coming back to bed.'

Briefly she thought of confiding in him and letting him deal with the matter. But she rejected the thought. Her head was invaded by confusion, and she wouldn't have known what to say.

In bed he took her back into his arms, comforting her with his warmth and strength. Seeking more, she ran her hands over him, taking reassurance from the feel of him. Suddenly she stopped.

'What is it?' he whispered.

She switched on the light and leaned back to survey his chest with the livid scar that ran across it. Slowly, almost fearfully, she touched it.

'That's what he did,' she murmured. 'Oh, God!' She laid her face against it.

'It's all right,' he said gently. 'It was bad at the time but they made me right again. I'm fine now. Don't grieve. It's over.'

'It's not over,' she wept. 'It'll never be over. You might have died.'

'I didn't die.'

But in another sense he had died, and so had she. The wounds had healed but the scars would be there for ever, and they both knew it. Through the barrier of time, from prison, from beyond the grave, Jake had put the shackles back on her.

Darius's wedding was drawing near. Back in Paris, Cassie booked them both into The Conway Hotel on Herringdean

Island. Freya called to say she would be there, but not Amos, which was a relief to them both.

'And my mother's coming,' Marcel said.

Since Laura Degrande also lived in Paris she would join them the night before their departure and travel with them. Cassie was curious to meet her, but also a little apprehensive, wondering what Marcel would have told her. Laura greeted her civilly but was not forthcoming. Sometimes Cassie would look up to find Marcel's mother watching her. Then Laura would smile, but not speak.

Between herself and Marcel, recent events were never mentioned. She shut him, and all to do with him, away in a compartment of her mind, which she bolted, barred, and threw away the key.

Marcel too never spoke of that time. He might have been waiting for a signal from her, which never came. With the wedding coming up they both assumed a cheerful demeanour. Nor was it entirely a pretence. She discovered that a locked compartment could work well, even if only intermittently.

Since it wasn't possible to take the train to Herringdean they travelled by helicopter and Cassie forgot her fear in the dazzling pleasure of skimming low over the Channel and seeing the island come into view.

'How beautiful,' she murmured.

'Yes, you really have to envy Darius,' Marcel agreed.

'Living in a place like this? I agree.'

'I meant more than that,' he murmured.

She turned her head and found him looking at her with a mysterious smile, but the helicopter was descending and there was no time to talk.

Darius was waiting as they landed, with a cheerful young woman by his side. Cassie took to Harriet at once.

Darius seemed on good terms with Laura, whom he hugged. After the introductions he said, 'I'll drive you to the hotel. When you've settled in, you come on to my place. We're having a big party.'

'Who else is here?' Marcel called.

'Jackson's arrived, and Travis. Travis is staying with me so that he can hide. He daren't go out in the street without girls shrieking, *"That's him!"* Jackson ribs him something terrible. They've started showing his series on Herringdean now, so there's no escape.'

'But not Amos,' Laura said. 'You assured me—'

'No, not Amos. Promise.'

They got through the hotel formalities as fast as possible, and were taken straight to Giant's Beacon, where Darius lived, which turned out to be a magnificent building overlooking the sea. They arrived to find Jackson and Travis standing outside, watching for them.

She recognised Travis at once as the actor she'd seen on screen. He greeted her with charm and practised friendliness, and she immediately understood why Freya was wary of him. Too charming. Too handsome.

She also recognised Jackson as a naturalist she'd seen on-screen. Not handsome in the Travis style, but good-looking in a 'kid brother' fashion. She liked him.

The house was decked out with flowers in the halls and one huge room filled with tables. Because this had to be saved for the wedding reception the next day, the family gathered outside that night and partied under lights hanging from the trees.

The Falcon family might be riven with divisions, but tonight they were forgotten and only the warmth could be felt. Cassie thought that Harry, as everyone called her, was exactly as a bride should be, full of happiness at her love but, more than that, the deep contentment of someone who knew, beyond all possible doubt, that she had come to the right place.

'When did you know for sure?' she asked when they were alone for a moment.

'It was him,' Harry said, pointing to a large dog who lay curled up on the sofa.

'Is that Phantom?' Cassie asked. 'Darius said he'd done a lot to bring you together, and you wanted him at the wedding.'

'That's right. We thought he was going to die one day, and I was called out on the lifeboat. I hated leaving him to die without me, but Darius stayed with him, talking to him, letting him know he was loved and wanted. And he didn't die. I still have my darling Phantom, and it's all because of Darius. I'd been wondering about him for a while, but that was the turning point, when it all became clear.'

Cassie nodded. 'If you were lucky enough to have a turning point everything would be easy,' she mused.

'Of course most people aren't that lucky,' Harry agreed. 'They have to just hope they've got it right. But I knew then that I mustn't let this wonderful man get away. When you find a man who understands you so perfectly you've got to hold onto him.'

'Yes,' Cassie murmured. 'If he understood you, and you understood him—everything would be simple.'

She reached down and stroked Phantom's head, wishing that she too could have a Phantom instead of the unruly ghosts who seemed bent on confusing her.

There was an excited murmur in the hall.

'That'll be Leonid,' Harry said. 'Darius went to collect him. He's the mystery man of the family, and I'm dying to meet him.'

From the first moment Leonid lived up to the tag 'mystery man'. He had black hair, dark blue eyes and an ultra-lean face.

'Haunted,' Cassie murmured. 'Or am I being too melodramatic?'

'I don't think so,' Harry murmured back.

Freya joined in. 'Where has he come from and where is he going?' she said. 'The rest of the world will never know.'

'Oh, that's really being a bit fanciful,' Harry protested.

'No,' said Freya. 'It isn't.'

The other two women exchanged glances that said, *Maybe he's the one she'll marry. This is going to be interesting.*

Watching Leonid make the rounds, Cassie had the impression that he knew none of his family well. She wondered how often he left Russia. He greeted her courteously, speaking in a deep voice with a distinctive accent. He was an attractive man, she thought, but very reserved, which some women might find intriguing.

Cassie suddenly realised that Laura was looking at her, then towards the trees with a question in her face. She nodded and rose, moving quietly away from the lights and under the trees, where she waited for Marcel's mother, who joined her a moment later.

'I have wanted to meet you for some time,' she said.

'Yes, I suppose Marcel has told you all about me. You must hate me.'

'I did once,' Laura agreed, 'many years ago. He came flying home from London, ran to me and shut himself away in his room. I used to stand outside the door and hear him sobbing. When he told me how his beautiful girlfriend had betrayed him when he was ill, then I hated you.

'I hated you even more as the years passed and I saw my generous, gentle son retreat into himself and turn into a terrible copy of his father. But a few weeks ago he came back home and found the letter. I saw his distress when he discovered pieces missing. It mattered so much to him. I wonder if you can understand how much it meant.

'When he was back in Paris he called me to say he'd spoken to you and all was now well. You had never betrayed him, and he could have known that if he hadn't torn up the letter. I've never heard him so happy. I thought soon he would tell me that you were reunited, but there has been nothing. And I came to ask you—to beg you—please don't break his heart again.'

'I don't want to, but—'

'But you're not sure you love him?'

'How can I be when I don't know who he is? We've both changed in ten years. I love—part of him, but the other part worries me. You said he'd become like his father. I need to know how much before I can make a decision.

'He's compared it to Jekyll and Hyde, and he's right. There are two people living inside each of us, and we all four have to learn to love each other. Otherwise there will only be more heartbreak and misery.'

'It will happen,' Laura said earnestly. 'It must. Look.' She reached into her bag and pulled out a little black box which she opened, revealing a ring with the biggest diamond Cassie had ever seen.

'Amos gave it to me when I first knew him. I've kept it all these years for Marcel, so that he can give it to the girl he loves.'

'It's beautiful,' Cassie said, gazing at the ring.

'Would you like to try it on?'

'No,' she said quickly. 'You're very kind but no thank you.'

Laura sighed and put the ring away. 'I shall hope for better things soon.'

As they strolled back together Jackson came out to call, 'Come on in! You'll never guess who's on the box *again!*'

'Travis?' Cassie laughed.

'Honestly, I swear he thinks he really comes from heaven. There's no getting away from him.'

In fact the episode was nearly over and they arrived just in time to hear Travis announce heroically, 'That's what we must all remember. Seize the moment whenever it comes. Don't let the chance slip away, or we may regret it for ever.'

Everyone in the room laughed and cheered, Travis looked sheepish and held out his glass for another drink.

Cassie cheered with the others, glancing across at Marcel to see if he shared the amusement, but he seemed sunk in thought, as though something had taken him by surprise.

But then he looked up and smiled. Someone appeared at Cassie's side, offering wine, and the party engulfed her again.

It was only later that she remembered Travis's dramatic pronouncement, because of its devastating consequences.

Next morning the family gathered on the beach for the wedding to take place. When Harry appeared she was accompanied by Darius's children, his daughter Frankie and son Mark. With them came Phantom, whom Mark led to the front and settled him where he had a good view.

Cassie watched, entranced, not only by the beauty of the ceremony and the surroundings, but by the love that blazed from the bride and groom.

She remembered Harry's words about the turning point, the moment when the road ahead became clear. Would she and Marcel ever reach that point? Or was it too much to hope for?

She stole a glance at him and found him looking at her intently. She smiled, receiving his smile in return. And something else? Had she imagined it or had he nodded? And if so, what had he meant?

Then he looked away, and she was left with her thoughts.

For a long time after that she wondered about that moment, and how differently everything might have turned out.

The reception was much as expected—speeches, laughter, happiness. Then they spilled out into the garden again and someone put on some music so that there could be dancing.

'Are you glad we came?' Marcel asked as they twirled under the trees.

'I wouldn't have missed it for the world. Everything was perfect.'

'Yes, they seized the chance when it came. Travis was right. That's what we should always do. Now, watch this!'

Plunging a hand into his pocket, he drew out the diamond ring Cassie had last seen in Laura's hand. Before she knew what he meant to do, he took her hand and slid it onto her finger.

'Marcel—'

'Seize the moment,' he said. 'This is our moment and I'm seizing it. *Listen, everybody!*'

They all stopped and looked at him eagerly.

'I've got wonderful news,' he cried. He held up Cassie's hand so that they could all see the glittering diamond.

'She's said yes, and the wedding will be as soon as possible.'

Cheers and applause. The family crowded around them, smiling, patting them on the back, embracing Cassie, asking to see the ring.

She showed it mechanically. Inwardly she was in turmoil, her mind whirling with a thousand desperate thoughts, of which the chief one was, *No!*

CHAPTER TWELVE

THE crowd waved and cheered. Harry flung her arms around Cassie, crying, 'You next. I'm so glad.'

Cassie maintained a determined smile, practically fixed on with rivets to hide her real thoughts.

She loved this man, so why wasn't she over the moon at his declaration of love?

Because there had been no such declaration, only a pronouncement without asking her opinion first. And this was the side of him that roused her hostility.

It would take a heart of stone to resist the way Marcel was gazing at her now, but she forced her heart to be stone.

'Aren't you going to ask me to dance?' she said and he swept her onto the floor.

Here there was a kind of safety. Nobody could hear them or study their whirling forms too closely.

'Well,' he said, smiling in a way that would have dazzled her with delight at any other time, 'we finally got that settled.'

'Did we?' she retorted. 'You didn't even wait for my reply.'

'I didn't need to,' he said, still smiling. 'I won't take no for an answer.'

Give in, cried a voice deep inside her. *You love him. Isn't that enough?*

But it wasn't enough to quell the indignation rising in her.

'But I won't have to, will I?' he persisted. 'You know this is what we both want.'

'If you're so sure of that, why won't you wait for me to answer?'

He sighed, humouring her. 'All right, we'll do it your way. Cassie my love, will you marry me?'

She looked into his eyes and shook her head. 'No, Marcel, I won't.'

'Oh, I see, you're going to make me beg.'

'No, don't beg. It would only make it worse when you have to accept my refusal.'

'Darling—'

'I mean it. Let's get out of here.'

The way back to the village lay along a road overlooking the sea. Halfway there, he stopped the car.

'Better if we talk here,' he said.

'Yes.' She left the car and went to stand looking out over the waves. 'I can't marry you, Marcel.'

'I know we've needed time to sort things out, but I thought we'd managed that by now.'

'But you didn't ask me. You just assumed I agreed with you and claimed me in front of everyone, almost as though the decision didn't concern me. That's the side of you I dislike so much, the side that makes you check up on me when I'm out, making phone calls to see if I'm there.'

'I never give up something that belongs to me. If it's mine, it's mine. You belong to me, and I won't give you up.'

'You talk as though I was an inanimate object, nothing but a possession.'

'You are a possession, but not inanimate. You belong to me because you once gave yourself to me of your own free will.'

'And then took myself back.'

'But not of your own free will. You yourself told me that, so it doesn't invalidate your original gift.'

'But you can't—we can't—'

'Maybe you can't, but I can. And I'm going to. All those years ago we made a verbal contract and I'm holding you to it.'

She regarded him with disbelief. She didn't know this man. He called himself Marcel, but there was a glint in his eyes that took her by surprise. It might almost have been humour, and the curve of his lips suggested a hint of teasing that went back to the other Marcel, years ago.

'A contract is a contract,' he said. 'You told me a thousand times that you belonged to me and nobody else. Nothing that's happened since invalidates that, so the deal still stands.'

'And that's what I am to you—a business arrangement.'

'Of course. But you'll find that I conduct business at very close quarters.' As he spoke he drew her close.

It was sweet to be in his arms again, but the voice of reason rose up and screamed, reminding her of all the sensible resolutions she'd made.

'No,' she said, pushing him away. 'Can't you understand? *No!*'

He stepped back. 'Then you don't love me?'

She sighed. 'Cassie loves you, but Mrs Henshaw can't stay with a man who behaves like this.'

'Isn't it time we forgot that Jekyll and Hyde nonsense?'

'But it's how things are, except that I'm content to be both people. But you aren't content. You only want one of us and you can't accept that we come as a package. But so do you. You're just as much two people as I am. One of you is the Marcel I loved. The other one acts more like Amos, or even J—'

'Don't!' he shouted. 'Don't dare to compare me to Jake Simpson.'

'Why not? He used to give me orders, and drive me up a blind alley so that there was no choice but to do as he wanted.'

Silence. Only the wind and the murmur of the waves.

'You'd better take this,' she said, handing him the ring. 'It might have fitted me years ago, but not now.'

By common consent, not a word was spoken as they returned to the hotel. Laura was already there.

'I didn't expect you two back so soon,' she teased.

'I'm tired,' Cassie said quickly. 'I'm going straight to bed.'

Laura's eager questioning look was more than she could endure. There was no way she could talk about what was happening, so she went quickly to her room and locked the door. Tonight she needed to be alone, perhaps to think, or perhaps to yield herself up to the confusion and dismay that was now all she could feel. She longed to go to sleep but could only stare up at the ceiling, longing for the night to be over.

Next day they all returned to Paris. Marcel drove Laura back to her home.

'Did you tell her?' Cassie asked when he returned.

'No. I wasn't sure what to say.'

'Tell her everything when I've left. I think I should go to London tomorrow.'

'And that's it?' he asked, aghast.

'When you see the end of the road there's nothing to do but head for it.'

'But is that really the end of the road? Cassie—'

'Don't,' she begged. 'I can't make you happy, Marcel, any more than you could make me happy. We're each of us too different from what the other wants.'

'Is that really true?' he whispered. 'I can't make you happy?'

Dumbly she shook her head.

It was as though someone had struck him a blow. He sagged, his head drooped and he turned away in defeat. Cassie reached out her hand, driven by the impulse to comfort him. But then she drew back. She had to stick to her resolve for both their sakes.

She spent the rest of the day alone in her room, tying up ends, leaving him notes. The night was sleepless. Every moment she expected him to come to her.

But he did not. He had accepted her decision.

Nor did he come next morning, and she wondered if he was going to let her go without another word. But there were surely words to be spoken at the last. She went along to his apartment and found Vera just leaving.

'He's given me the day off,' she said. 'Bye!'

She sped along the corridor and Cassie slipped inside. There was no sign of Marcel. She closed her eyes, full of confusion. Her mind and heart were full of so many feelings and impressions, and they all seemed to contradict each other.

She looked into the bedroom which, by now, she knew, with its extra large double bed that was so comfortable for the indulgence of pleasure followed by sleep. But he wasn't there. Next stood another door which she'd only half noticed before. She tried the handle and felt it give.

Probably a cupboard, she thought, easing it open, meaning just to take a quick glance. But what she found made her push the door wide and stand on the threshold, confused and trying desperately to understand.

It was a bedroom, although prison cell might have described it better. Pushed up against the wall was a bed so narrow that it sent a dismal message. No lovers could ever share that restricted space. The man who slept here slept alone. There was no wardrobe. A small bedside chest of drawers was the only other furniture.

But surely, she thought, Marcel slept in the huge bed in the other room? But this one looked as if it had been recently slept in, and only clumsily made. It couldn't be anyone but him, which meant—surely not?

She sensed the truth by instinct. The outer room was the bedroom 'for show', the place where he took good-time girls who would expect to find him sleeping in lush surroundings, no expense spared. To keep up his reputation, he provided the background they expected, wined and dined them, made the speeches they would expect of a playboy and seduced them

But then he retreated to this bleak little place, because this was where he felt he belonged. Here he could be his true self. At least, that was how he felt.

The warm, life-loving, open-hearted boy she had loved had become the man who only felt truly comfortable in retreat. That thought distressed her more than any other.

And he'd loved the same about her, she thought, remembering how he'd said only recently, 'She gave herself to the world.'

They had both changed, both been damaged. She had thought she understood the extent of the injury to him, but now she was being forced to recognise how badly he'd been hurt.

'So now you know,' said a voice behind her.

Turning, she saw Marcel in the doorway, watching her. She searched his face for anger but found only weariness and resignation.

'Why didn't you tell me?' she whispered, gesturing to the bleak surroundings.

'Why do you think? Do you imagine I wanted you to know what a hopeless, miserable specimen I'd become? Look at it!'

'It…doesn't look very comfortable,' she said, searching for the right words.

'It doesn't need to be comfortable. It serves its purpose.'

She couldn't bear any more. She put her arms about him in an embrace of comfort. She thought he would cling to her, but at first he didn't. Instead his hands reached up hesitantly, barely touching her, then down again, as though he wasn't quite sure.

But at last he seemed to summon up his courage, wrapping his arms about her, drawing her against him and dropping his head so that his face was hidden against her neck. Cassie stroked his hair softly and they stood like that for a long time.

'I usually keep this door locked,' he said. 'Nobody else has any idea. Nobody ever will.'

'Nobody?' she asked.

'Nobody at all. This is me, deep inside, where nobody else ever gets to look. Not since…well…'

She stroked his face. 'Oh, my dear, dear Marcel—how long have you had this?'

'Since I bought the hotel, five years ago. Out there is the "official bedroom", and in here is the real one.'

'You never brought me in here.'

'I was waiting for the right moment—' He looked at her.

'It's now,' she said, drawing him down.

In the narrow bed there was only one way to make love, and that was to cling together, arms holding each other close, faces touching gently. When he claimed her she felt herself become one with him as never before. When he'd finished she offered herself to him again, and felt him accept her gift gratefully. In return he gave her gifts of power and tenderness that made her heart rejoice as never before in her life.

As the storm died away and she felt peace return she knew a passionate gratitude that this had happened while there was still time.

She looked up at him, eyes shining with love, waiting for him to utter the words that would start their life together.

'Goodbye,' he said.

* * *

Later that day he took her to the airport.

'There's the line for Check In,' he said. 'You're in good time. I'll go now.'

She turned tortured eyes towards him.

'Don't worry,' he said. 'I won't trouble you any more. I'm glad we had this morning. It means we can part on good terms, and that's important after the way we parted last time.'

He was silent, searching her face for something he needed to find there.

'At least we met again and found out…well, things we needed to find out. We'll always have that.'

'Marcel—'

'I told you it's all right. You're free of me now. No one stalking you, checking up on you, trying to back you into a corner. You were right about that. Goodbye, my darling. Be happy.'

'And you,' she said.

'Happy? Without you? Surely you understand that the only happiness I can have now is knowing that I set you free. Heaven forbid that you should regard me as you regarded him, a bully who forced you to do what he wanted. It's the way I was going, wasn't it? I wouldn't face it, but it was true. Thank goodness you showed me in time.'

'Why did it have to be this way?' she whispered.

'I don't know, but I do know that if we'd stayed together you'd have come to hate me, and I'll endure anything but that. Goodbye, my dearest. Find a man who deserves you, and be happy with him.'

'You can wish that?' she asked, amazed.

'I can wish anything for you that's good.'

'And you—oh, heavens, we both harmed each other so much. If only—'

'I know. But I won't risk harming you any more.' He leaned down and kissed her cheek. 'Goodbye.'

She watched as he walked away. Last time they had been in this airport he'd cried out her name in desperate determination to stop her leaving. But now he kept walking, not once looking back.

She stood there for a long, long time before moving off very slowly.

She was numb for the journey. Only when she was at home, behind a locked door, staring into the darkness, did she finally face what had happened.

Marcel had opened his arms and set her free because it was the only way he could show himself better than her fears. By doing this he'd proved the strength of his love for her.

It was the moment she'd been secretly waiting for, what Harry had called 'the turning point, when it all became clear.'

The clarity was blinding. Marcel had done what she hadn't believed possible, behaving with a generosity that paradoxically freed her to love him completely. Now she knew beyond all doubt that he was the one. The only one.

And she had lost him. It was over. Final.

Perhaps it was the best thing for him too, she thought, trying to comfort herself. If they had stayed together she might have made him wretched. He deserved better than that. He deserved better than *her*.

And with the thought came a sense of pride and even happiness that she'd thought never to know again. Marcel had loved her enough to ignore his own needs, his own pain. His generosity raised him head and shoulders above all other men. To be loved by him was an honour.

She might never see or hear from him again, but as long as she lived she would know that she'd won the heart of the finest, bravest, strongest, most honourable man in the world. That thought would sustain her throughout the long, sad years ahead.

* * *

Back in London, she realised that it was time to be practical. She was out of a job. There was more in her bank account than she had realised, owing to a sudden infusion of funds from Paris on the day she'd left. Marcel had put in three months' wages as a farewell gift.

She texted him, *Thank you.* And received in return, *Good luck!*

Nothing else. Not a word.

But the money wouldn't last for ever, as she realised when she visited her family, and her brother-in-law exclaimed, 'Do you mean you're out of a job?'

'Don't worry,' she said, handing him a cheque. 'I'll get another.'

But what? That was the question. The business world beckoned, but it no longer satisfied her. She needed more to fill the emptiness inside.

A few evenings later she went for a walk along the Thames, sometimes stopping to lean on the wall and watch the blazing sunset over the river. As she gazed she suddenly heard the sound of a familiar click, and turned to see a man aiming a camera at her.

'Don't move,' he called. 'I haven't finished.'

'You've got a cheek,' she began, then stopped. 'Hey, aren't you—Toby?'

Toby had been the eager young assistant of the photographer who had helped to make Cassie's name ten years ago. Since then he'd become successful on his own account.

'How lovely to see you after all this time!' she said, embracing him warmly. 'Let's go and have a coffee.'

'Not just yet,' he said. 'I'm not passing up my chance of a photo session with the great Cassie.'

'She's not the great Cassie any more. Let's get back to the studio.'

The pictures astonished her so much that she yielded readily to his suggestion of a 'proper shoot'. It was simple fun until he said, 'I've had a brilliant idea. The return of Cassie, more beautiful than ever.'

'You're mad,' she said, laughing.

'Sure I'm mad. That's what's most fun. Now, here's what we'll do…'

Her return was a sensation. Voluptuous Cassie belonged to the past. This was another age, Toby told her. Lean and boyish was 'in'. Now she was in demand again.

One evening a few weeks later, there was a knock at her door and she opened to find—

'Freya!'

When they were both settled over tea and cakes, Freya said, 'I hear you're making a modelling comeback.'

'Not really. Just a few shoots. I simply wanted to be sure I could do it.'

'Cassie still lives, huh?'

'Yes, she does. That was a nice surprise, and Mrs Henshaw thinks the money's nice, so we'll see. What about you?'

'I've come back to London to get a nursing job. Amos was just getting too much for me. You'll never guess what his latest wheeze is.'

'Jackson? Leonid? Travis?'

'Still Marcel. Honestly, that man doesn't understand the word "no". He's only put a load of money into my bank account, without even asking me. He knows Marcel needs money and he thought that would sway him.'

'Why is he still in need of money? I thought that was all sorted.'

'So did Amos. He was going to squeeze it out of that man—remember him?'

'I remember,' Cassie said quietly.

'But Marcel made him back off.'

'Marcel did?' Cassie asked quickly.

'Yes, I gather there were some very tough discussions and Marcel prevailed. So then they needed money from somewhere else, and he's raised it by selling shares in La Couronne.'

'But that place is his pride and joy!'

'Yes, but his mind was made up. He raised the cash and he's bought the London hotel but he's not out of the woods yet. So Amos thought making me rich would make Marcel go down on one knee.'

'And you don't think it will?' Cassie asked, pouring tea with great concentration.

'I've warned him if he does I'll thump him. Besides, he's still pining for you.'

A pause while her heart lurched, then a shaky laugh. 'That's nonsense.'

'No, it's not. I called in on him in Paris on my way here and we had a talk. He told me how your engagement ended. Not that there was really an engagement, was there? What an idiot he was to do it that way! I told him what I thought of him. But you two are right for each other and I won't see it come to nothing just because he's made a stupid mistake.'

Cassie shook her head helplessly. 'It's too late for that.'

'You mean you don't love him any more?'

'Of course I love him. I always will, but—'

'Do you want to talk?' Freya asked.

'Yes, I need to. When I first returned to London I was sad at losing Marcel, but I could bear it because I was so proud of him for leaving me. He did it to protect me. I'm still proud of him but—'

'But there's a lot of life still to get through,' Freya said shrewdly.

'I want him back, but I can't try to tempt him back. That's not the way.'

'Right, because if he could be tempted you wouldn't still be proud of him,' Freya said.

'Right. You're so clever. I really wish you were my sister.'

'If we play our cards right, I soon will be. Tempting is out. Compulsion is in. You've got to grab him by the scruff of the neck and not give him any choice. Now, listen carefully. This is what we're going to do...'

A few weeks later Vera glanced up as her employer hurried in. His face was tense and troubled, as always these days. But she thought that might be about to change.

'You have a visitor,' she said. 'Someone has just bought some shares in this place and says they need to see you urgently.' She nodded in the direction of her office door. 'In there.'

Frowning, he went in and stopped on the threshold.

'Hello,' said Cassie.

He drew a long breath, fighting for the control that he would need at this moment more than any other. 'What... Vera said...shareholder...'

'That's right. I've bought shares in La Couronne and I thought I should tell you soon.'

'But...it must have cost you a fortune. How did you—?'

'Raise the cash? From Freya. She's made me a big loan, which I shall pay off from the money I'll make from the hotel.'

'But surely she can't have loaned you enough to—'

'No, I have another source of income. That time we visited Jake, he sneakily returned my ring to me, the one he gave me just before we married. I found it in my bag afterwards, and now I've sold it, and I've invested the money in you.

'It's only for a short while. I don't want to keep anything of his permanently. His ring sold for nearly half a million. As soon as I can afford it I'll give an equal amount to charity. By then, Jake will have served his purpose.'

'Bringing you back to me,' he murmured.

'Exactly. Jake separated us, and now Jake has helped us find each other again.'

'He'd hate that,' Marcel said with relish.

'Yes, that's the thought I enjoy most. My other source of income is this.'

She opened a magazine, displaying Cassie, centrefold. She was stretched out, in a tiny bikini, looking directly into the camera with eyes that were almost as seductive as her barely clothed body.

'Take a good look,' she purred.

'I don't need to. I have my own copy. I'm amazed. I thought Mrs Henshaw had taken over.'

'So do the people I deal with, until they learn their mistake. It's Cassie who poses but Mrs Henshaw who draws up Cassie's contracts. They're the best of friends now.'

'I'm glad to know that,' he said carefully. 'It could make life…a lot easier.'

'It certainly does. Cassie's going to have to flaunt herself for quite a while yet, to help pay off Mrs Henshaw's debts, so the two of them decided to live together in harmony. Take one, you get the other.' She slipped her arms about his neck. 'I hope that's all right with you.'

It was hard to speak, but he managed to say, 'You once told me to get out of your life, and stay out.'

'That was then, this is now.'

He was suddenly tense. 'Cassie, my love, don't do this unless you mean it with all your heart. I couldn't endure to lose you again. I must be sure—to know that you're sure. I was torn from you once, and the last time I left you because it was the right thing to do. I thought it would help me keep your love, even if we could only love from a distance.'

'Yes, I understood that. I thought you were wonderful, even though losing you again broke my heart.'

'But—you said it yourself. That was then, this is now.' He met her eyes and spoke softly. 'Another parting would kill me.'

'There will be no other parting,' she vowed. 'I'm as sure as you want me to be, but sure in a way you don't know about yet. Things have changed. It's probably your influence. I'm not afraid of your controlling side because I've got one too. You brought it out in me and now it's out it's out for good.

'You need to know this. I'm in charge. From now on we're going to do things my way.' She laid her lips softly against his. 'Understand?'

'Understand.'

She could feel temptation trembling through him, making him draw back after a moment.

'You know that we'll fight,' he said.

'Of course we will. We'll have terrible fights, call each other all sorts of names, dig up our memories and use them to hurt each other. Sometimes we'll even hate each other. But we'll do it equally.'

'Oh, really? Well, let me tell you, conquering Cassie is a pleasure, but conquering Mrs Henshaw—that's something I'm really looking forward to.'

She smiled, nodding towards the door of the little bedroom.

'Better get started then. I don't know what you're waiting for.'

He lifted her high and headed for the door.

'Who's waiting?' he said.

* * * * *

CLASSIC

Quintessential, modern love stories
that are romance at its finest.

COMING NEXT MONTH
AVAILABLE MARCH 13, 2012

REQUEST YOUR FREE BOOKS!
2 FREE NOVELS PLUS 2 FREE GIFTS!

Harlequin®

Romance

From the Heart, For the Heart

YES! Please send me 2 FREE Harlequin® Romance novels and my 2 FREE gifts (gifts are worth about $10). After receiving them, if I don't wish to receive any more books, I can return the shipping statement marked "cancel". If I don't cancel, I will receive 6 brand-new novels every month and be billed just $4.09 per book in the U.S. or $4.49 per book in Canada. That's a savings of at least 14% off the cover price! It's quite a bargain! Shipping and handling is just 50¢ per book in the U.S. and 75¢ per book in Canada.* I understand that accepting the 2 free books and gifts places me under no obligation to buy anything. I can always return a shipment and cancel at any time. Even if I never buy another book, the two free books and gifts are mine to keep forever.

116/316 HDN FESE

Name	(PLEASE PRINT)	
Address		Apt. #
City	State/Prov.	Zip/Postal Code

Signature (if under 18, a parent or guardian must sign)

Mail to the Reader Service:
IN U.S.A.: P.O. Box 1867, Buffalo, NY 14240-1867
IN CANADA: P.O. Box 609, Fort Erie, Ontario L2A 5X3

Not valid for current subscribers to Harlequin Romance books.

Are you a subscriber to Harlequin Romance books and want to receive the larger-print edition?
Call 1-800-873-8635 or visit www.ReaderService.com.

* Terms and prices subject to change without notice. Prices do not include applicable taxes. Sales tax applicable in N.Y. Canadian residents will be charged applicable taxes. Offer not valid in Quebec. This offer is limited to one order per household. All orders subject to credit approval. Credit or debit balances in a customer's account(s) may be offset by any other outstanding balance owed by or to the customer. Please allow 4 to 6 weeks for delivery. Offer available while quantities last.

Your Privacy—The Reader Service is committed to protecting your privacy. Our Privacy Policy is available online at www.ReaderService.com or upon request from the Reader Service.

We make a portion of our mailing list available to reputable third parties that offer products we believe may interest you. If you prefer that we not exchange your name with third parties, or if you wish to clarify or modify your communication preferences, please visit us at www.ReaderService.com/consumerschoice or write to us at Reader Service Preference Service, P.O. Box 9062, Buffalo, NY 14269. Include your complete name and address.

HRI1B

USA TODAY bestselling author

Carol Marinelli

begins a daring duet.

THE SECRETS
of
XANOS

Two brothers alike in charisma and power;
separated at birth and seeking revenge…

Nico has always felt like an outsider. He's turned his back on his
parents' fortune to become one of Xanos's most powerful exports
and nothing will stand in his way—until he stumbles
upon a virgin bride….

Zander took his chances on the streets rather than spending another
moment under his cruel father's roof. Now he is unrivaled in
business—and the bedroom! He wants the best people around him,
and Charlotte is the best PA! Can he tempt her
over to the dark side…?

A SHAMEFUL CONSEQUENCE
Available in March

AN INDECENT PROPOSITION
Available in April

HP13053

New York Times *and* USA TODAY *bestselling author*
Maya Banks presents book three in her miniseries
PREGNANCY & PASSION.

TEMPTED BY HER INNOCENT KISS

Available March 2012 from Harlequin Desire!

There came a time in a man's life when he knew he was
well and truly caught. Devon Carter stared down at the diamond ring nestled in velvet and acknowledged that this was
one such time. He snapped the lid closed and shoved the
box into the breast pocket of his suit.

He had two choices. He could marry Ashley Copeland
and fulfill his goal of merging his company with Copeland
Hotels, thus creating the largest, most exclusive line of re-
sorts in the world, or he could refuse and lose it all.

Put in that light, there wasn't much he could do except
pop the question.

The doorman to his Manhattan high-rise apartment hurried to open the door as Devon strode toward the street.
He took a deep breath before ducking into his car, and the
driver pulled into traffic.

Tonight was the night. All of his careful wooing, the
countless dinners, kisses that started brief and casual and
became more breathless—all a lead-up to tonight. Tonight
his seduction of Ashley Copeland would be complete, and
then he'd ask her to marry him.

He shook his head as the absurdity of the situation hit
him for the hundredth time. Personally, he thought William
Copeland was crazy for forcing his daughter down Devon's
throat.

Ashley was a sweet enough girl, but Devon had no desire

to marry anyone.

William had other plans. He'd told Devon that Ashley had no head for the family business. She was too softhearted, too naive. So he'd made Ashley part of the deal. The catch? Ashley wasn't to know of it. Which meant Devon was stuck playing stupid games.

Ashley was supposed to think this was a grand love match. She was a starry-eyed woman who preferred her animal-rescue foundation over board meetings, charts and financials for Copeland Hotels.

If she ever found out the truth, she wouldn't take it well.

And hell, he couldn't blame her.

But no matter the reason for his proposal, before the night was over, she'd have no doubts that she belonged to him.

What will happen when Devon marries Ashley?
Find out in Maya Banks's passionate new novel
TEMPTED BY HER INNOCENT KISS
Available March 2012 from Harlequin Desire!